FLAMES OVER NORWAY

Robert Jackson

SEVERN SH HOUSE

This first world edition published in Great Britain 1996 by
SEVERN HOUSE PUBLISHERS LTD of
9–15 High Street, Sutton, Surrey SM1 1DF.
First published in the USA 1996 by
SEVERN HOUSE PUBLISHERS INC of
595 Madison Avenue, New York, NY 10022.

British Library Cataloguing in Publication Data
Jackson, Robert, 1941–
Flames over Norway
1. English fiction – 20th century
I. Title
823.9′14 [F]

ISBN 0-7278-4900-X

Typeset by Hewer Text Composition Services, Edinburgh.
Printed and bound in Great Britain by
Hartnolls Ltd, Bodmin, Cornwall.

Chapter One

From 20,000 feet the view was magnificent. From the cockpit, *Leutnant* Hans Lehmann could see most of the Danish peninsula as far as Esbjerg; beyond that, the land was lost in a summer heat haze.

He glanced across at his wingman, *Unteroffizier* Falcke, whose aircraft was 600 feet to the right and slightly astern. The Messerschmitt 109, shark-like and deadly, glittered in the sunlight; its upper surfaces were painted dark green, contrasting sharply with the pale blue of its undersides. The black, white-edged crosses on wings and fuselage sides, and the *Hakenkreuz* – the sinister Swastika symbol of the Third Reich – on the tail fin stood out starkly against the camouflage.

Falcke's Me 109, like the fighter Lehmann was flying, was a brand-new E-2 model, a big improvement over the Me 109B which both pilots had flown during the Spanish Civil War as part of the *Kondor* Legion – the military formation sent under conditions of great secrecy to the aid of the Spanish nationalist leader General Franco. That bitter, bloody war had provided an unparalleled opportunity to test the latest combat aircraft that were entering service with the *Reichsluftwaffe*, and to develop the tactics that would give Germany's pilots an advantage over their opponents in the war that now seemed inevitable.

The battle formation flown now by Lehmann and Falcke, was a product of the war in Spain; it enabled each pilot to cover the other's blind spots, especially the area behind and below the aircraft. If an attack took place on one of the pair, the other would warn him; the threatened aircraft would break hard outwards and the second fighter would break in the same direction, so that if the enemy pilot continued his attack on the turn he would soon find the second 109 on his tail. Lehmann had disposed of three Spanish Republican I-16 *Ratas* – tubby little Russian-built fighters – using this technique, and Falcke had bagged a couple more.

That had been a year ago, in the summer of 1938, during the closing months of the Spanish conflict. Lehmann had just scored his third victory when all remaining *Kondor* Legion personnel had been hurriedly recalled to Germany to face a threat of war that followed the *Anschluss*, the annexation of Austria. Lehmann was aware that not all Austrians had relished the idea of being incorporated into the *Reich* without having a say in the matter, while Britain and France had made warlike noises. But that was all they had done. The British and French had backed down at the conference table in Munich in September of 1938, their leaders following the path of appeasement. It had been an enormous political triumph for Germany's leader, Adolf Hitler, who had used the months that followed to build up his armed forces to an even greater pitch of material power and efficiency. War, Lehmann was sure, would still come – but only when the *Führer* chose to start it.

Lehmann opened the throttle slightly and applied left stick and rudder, swinging the Messerschmitt into a gentle turn. Falcke followed instantly, as though attached to his leader by a thread. Lehmann delighted in the 109's response to his touch, revelling in the surge of power that came with the new throttle setting, conscious of the reserve that still remained untapped beneath the fighter's long engine cowling.

The *Emil*, as the Me 109E was known to its pilots, had a Daimler-Benz DB 601A engine producing 1100 horsepower – one-third as much again as the power of the Junkers Jumo engines fitted in the earlier models. It gave the 109E a top speed of 350 miles per hour and an operational ceiling of 36,000 feet. Best of all, it was equipped with a new fuel injection system that kept it running even when the aircraft was upside down, so there was no longer a tendency for the engine to cut out during violent combat manoeuvres.

The armament was good, too: two MG FF 20-millimetre cannon and a pair of 7.62 mm machine-guns, providing a formidable punch that would knock down any adversary. It felt good to be sitting behind offensive power of that kind, available at the touch of a finger.

Lehmann held the 109 in the turn, watching the earth revolve slowly nearly four miles beneath his wings. The long chain of the East Friesian islands appeared ahead of the nose, winding away into the distance towards Germany's border with Holland. The islands drifted away to the right and the *Emil*'s nose pointed inland; down there, invisible from this altitude, was the airfield of Jever – the home base of Lehmann's unit, the famous *Jagdgeschwader* 77.

Lehmann was proud of the fact that JG 77 was one of the *Luftwaffe*'s élite fighter wings, which was reflected in its assignment: the air defence of north-west Germany and, in particular, of the vital naval base of Wilhelmshaven. The latter came into view now, a dark and smoky smudge on the horizon, nestling on the western shores of Jade Bay.

Lehmann continued to turn through a full circle of 360 degrees and then levelled out, his nose pointing north-westward in the direction of the island of Heligoland. Off his left wingtip, in the distance, was Wangerooge, the most easterly of the Friesians. That, or at least what was on it, was the main reason for the sortie being flown on this August morning. There was some sort of top secret installation down there, an apparatus that was supposed to give warning of hostile aircraft approaching the German coast from the North Sea. Its controllers, or whatever one would call them, were to have contacted him and given him and Falcke a series of courses to steer, presumably so that they could check out the effectiveness of their equipment. So far, there hadn't been a squeak out of the station, and calls from Lehmann on the assigned radio-frequency had met with no response. Well, he told himself, we'll give them another ten minutes, and then go home. Besides, fuel would soon be running low.

"Starling two to leader. Aircraft bearing two-six-zero, low and closing."

Falcke's broad Swabian accent, sounding loud in his headset, broke into Lehmann's thoughts. He looked down to the left and saw it almost immediately: the silvery cross of an aircraft, some 5000 feet lower down and heading directly for Jade Bay from the north-west. No camouflage, he thought, so almost certainly civilian; but this whole area had been restricted to military aircraft only for the past three weeks, so it had no business to be there.

"All right, Falcke, let's take a look."

He pushed over the stick and sent the Messerschmitt arrowing down towards the sea, followed closely by his wingman. Pulling out of the dive at 15,000 feet, the two 109s shot past the incoming aircraft and turned steeply through 180 degrees, approaching it from astern and throttling back to match its lower speed. Ordering Falcke to formate on its opposite side, Lehmann closed the gap until he was tucked in close to the civil aircraft's port wingtip.

He had already identified the intruder as a Heinkel He 70, a fast single-engined aircraft widely used for rapid communications and mail delivery. He recalled that one or two had been used experimentally in the reconnaissance role in Spain, and as a result of that experience they had equipped a few *Luftwaffe* recce units before being replaced by the more effective twin-engined Dornier Do 17 in 1938.

He scanned the sleek aircraft from nose to tail. Its silvery surfaces were highly polished, their uniformity broken only by a red band across the tail fin – the swastika in a white circle at its centre – and black civil registration letters, D-UBOF, on the fuselage side.

Lehmann became conscious that the Heinkel's pilot was looking at him. The man raised a hand and waved. Lehmann waved back, then made a gesture to indicate that the Heinkel must alter course to take it clear of the Jade. The pilot waved again to show that he had understood, and turned 30 degrees to port, so that he was now flying parallel to the north German coastline, skirting the outer limit of the restricted area.

Lehmann relaxed. He reasoned that the Heinkel pilot was probably bound for Hamburg, and that he had intended to take a short cut across the prohibited territory surrounding Wilhelmshaven. His new course would take him to the Elbe estuary, from where he would follow the river south to his destination.

The fighter pilot glanced at his fuel gauge, and saw that the needle was slipping towards the red danger mark. It was time to go home. He waggled his wings briefly, the gesture acknowledged by another wave from the Heinkel pilot, then put the *Emil* into a diving turn towards the coast and Jever, Falcke taking up his usual slot off the right wing.

Above them now, the pilot of the He 70 peered

over his right shoulder, craning his neck to see past the trailing edge of the wing. He watched the two Messerschmitts as they dived, following them until they vanished in the blue haze. Then, letting out his breath in a long explosion of relief, he abruptly turned the nose of his aircraft through 90 degrees until it was pointing due north towards international waters. The haze was thickening now, and at this height the Heinkel would be invisible from the surface.

He reached out a gloved hand and flicked a switch. Concealed in the Heinkel's belly, a high-resolution camera stopped rolling. The pilot held a northerly course for a few more miles, until the appearance of Heligoland dead ahead told him that it was time to turn again. He did so, and this time the Heinkel's nose swung round until it was pointing towards the west.

Far below and a long way behind, the two Me 109s flattened out on their approach to land at Jever. As his aircraft's wheels bounced over the grass, Lehmann wondered idly where the Heinkel had come from; but it was no more than a passing thought.

If he had thought a little more deeply, and retraced the course that the Heinkel had been following when it was first sighted, he would have realized that the line would lead to only one possible point of departure – a point that was not on the German side of the North Sea.

Chapter Two

Armstrong spotted the sign with a mixture of relief and annoyance. Relief, because he was now more or less certain of his bearings; annoyance, because he must have ridden past the sign at least twice in the past half-hour without seeing it. He consoled himself, though not much, with the thought that the rain had robbed him of his power of observation.

The sign, which was not very large, spelled out DEANLAND AERO CLUB. There was a small arrow underneath, pointing up a narrow side road that was little more than a cart-track. Grass grew up the middle of it and there were tall, tangled hedgerows on either side.

Well, he thought, his orders were to report to Deanland Aerodrome, and where there was an aero club there must be an airfield. He turned his powerful 633 cc Norton motor cycle – his pride and joy, and one from which his bank balance was only just recovering – into the narrow road and proceeded with caution, for the road was winding. From what he could see, to judge by the tortuous line of roadside trees up ahead, it continued to wind for a long way.

He was tired and wet, and his spirits were not

at their highest level. They rose only the merest fraction when the rain ceased abruptly in a flurry of shining drops and the summer sun shot out from behind a bank of cloud. For the umpteenth time he wondered what was in store for him, and why he had been ordered to this godforsaken spot in darkest East Anglia. The sudden move had, to say the least, come as a severe shock to his system. He could still hardly credit that it was only a day since his squadron adjutant had handed him the signal from the Air Ministry, no less, ordering him to report forthwith to a place he'd never even heard of. Already, the heady pride of belonging to one of Fighter Command's first – and foremost – Spitfire squadrons seemed no more than a dim memory.

He was mystified, too, by the stipulation in his orders that he was to report to Deanland in civilian clothing, and this at a time when the entire nation was moving rapidly into uniform to meet the war that everyone knew was inevitable, even though millions who had lived through the last one prayed that it might still be avoided. Armstrong and his fellow pilots had known the possibility of it ever since Hitler's Germany had annexed Austria, and when the Nazis marched into Czechoslovakia a few months later the possibility had turned to certainty.

That had been in March 1939. It was now August, and there was no doubt left in anyone's mind what Hitler's next target would be. And if he invaded Poland, the British Prime Minister, Neville Chamberlain, had already announced that

Britain would stand by the Poles. War, as the young pilots of Armstrong's squadron had discussed with an eagerness born of their youth, could only be a matter of weeks – perhaps days – away. They had reached a peak of operational efficiency, and now they wanted to see combat. They would give the Huns a trouncing.

And Flying Officer Kenneth Armstrong, heading for the middle of nowhere, was likely to see none of it. Deanland he knew nothing about, except for the certain fact that it was not a fighter station. He didn't even know if it belonged to the RAF.

He rode on for a mile and a half, between rows of tall elms. In the distance, he glimpsed an occasional farm, nestling amid wooded Suffolk hillsides across which cloud shadows chased one another. And then he saw the windsock, an orange sleeve fluttering in the breeze at the end of a tall pole.

Armstrong rounded a series of sharp bends and entered a straight stretch of road. It led to a gate; the windsock's pole was planted some distance away on the right. He slowed and came to a stop in the gateway, inspecting another sign that ordered all vehicles to follow a track that ran round the perimeter of a large grass field. On the opposite side of the field, directly opposite, he could see a couple of long huts and two hangars. One of them he identified as the type known as a *Bessoneau*, erected in large numbers during the 1914–18 war; the other seemed to be a wooden structure, doubtless dating from the same period. No aircraft were visible, and there wasn't a soul in sight. His spirits plummeted again; if this was any kind of operational station there would surely have been signs of activity, not to mention armed guards.

Resignedly, Armstrong set off round the perimeter track, heading for the nearer hangar – the wooden one – and taking stock of things as he went. The low hedge that surrounded the airfield was neatly and recently trimmed, which suggested that somebody was looking after the place, and the grass itself was cut short. He could smell the aroma of it, coaxed from the damp ground by the sunlight.

There was bound to be someone about, he thought, as he headed along the stretch of track that appeared to end at the hangar. Before long, maybe he would have the answers to a growing list of questions.

A shadow flashed over him and he looked up, startled, almost losing control of his motor cycle. He slewed to a stop, cutting his engine and craning his neck to see the aircraft that roared overhead, its cockpit canopy flashing as it turned, reflecting the sunlight. It had an elliptical wing shape, and for a confused second Armstrong thought that it was a Spitfire, but he realized almost instantly that he was mistaken. He had seen the type before, but for the life of him he couldn't think where. He racked his brain as the strange aircraft completed a circuit of the field and levelled out into wind, its engine burbling as it came down to land, its undercarriage lowered.

Mentally, Armstrong checked off details as the aircraft rounded out and touched down, bouncing slightly on its mainwheels before it lost speed and finally settled as its tail came down. It had a long cockpit behind its single engine and was much larger than a Spitfire, with a wingspan, he guessed, of about 50 feet. It was silver overall and looked extremely smart, but that was not the fact about it that struck Armstrong. What did strike him, as the aircraft turned broadside on to him as it taxied towards the larger hangar, was the solitary marking it carried, a splash of colour against the silver finish. Emblazoned on the aircraft's tail was a broad, red horizontal band. And in the middle of the red band, standing out starkly against a white circle, was the black swastika of the Third Reich.

Suddenly, Armstrong recalled where he had seen this aircraft before. Its silhouette had stared out at him from a recognition poster of German types, pinned to the wall of his squadron's dispersal hut. It was a Heinkel He 70.

Fascinated and intrigued, he brought his cycle back to life and rode up to the hangar, where he dismounted and propped it on its stand near the side wall. As he did so, the Heinkel's pilot gunned the engine briefly to clear surplus oil from the plugs and then switched off, bringing silence back to the airfield.

The Heinkel's cockpit canopy slid back. Armstrong watched the pilot unfasten his seat harness and lever himself out on to the wing; intent on the aircraft and its occupant, he only half noticed that the hangar doors were starting to open, manipulated by someone inside. The pilot, who wore a white overall, paused on the wing for a moment to take off his flying helmet, then jumped down from the trailing edge onto the grass. He signalled to whoever was in the hangar, and a moment later four men in khaki overalls emerged at a run and began to push the Heinkel towards the hangar, whose doors were now fully open.

The pilot, meanwhile, advanced towards Armstrong, who stood there filled with incredulity as recognition hit him with a jolt. It was more than three years since he had last seen Wing Commander Horace Royston, but even if it had been 20 he would not have forgotten the more senior officer's tall, aristocratic figure. Royston was a character straight out of the pages of the *Boy's Own Paper*, a typical upper-crust Englishman of the kind who had made his mark from the snows of the Himalayas to the torrid jungles of Africa. The caricature was complete, right down to the dark hair brushed straight back and parted in the middle and the small, neatly-trimmed moustache.

Royston stuck out his hand, smiling rather secretively. Armstrong thought that he looked tired, and noticed that there were patches of sweat on his flying overall.

"Good to see you again, Armstrong," he said. "Do hope you didn't have any trouble finding the place. It's a bit off the map."

"Not at all, sir," Armstrong lied, shaking the proffered hand briefly. "Can't help wondering what it's all about, though." He inclined his head towards the hangar, into which the Heinkel had now disappeared. Royston's smile widened into a grin.

"All in good time," he said, glancing at his watch. "Four-thirty. I expect you could do with a cup of tea. I certainly could." He pointed to the Norton. "Is that your kit strapped to the back of that thing?"

Armstrong nodded. "Leave it there," Royston told him. "I'll have someone take it to your room. Facilities are a bit basic here, I'm afraid, but I expect you'll get used to the occasional shortage of hot water."

Royston turned and led Armstrong past the front of the hangar towards one of the long huts. As they walked, the newcomer reflected on the last time their paths had crossed. It had been in the spring of 1936, when Armstrong – then a pilot officer – had been seconded for a few weeks to an experimental establishment at Farnborough, where a small staff under Royston's leadership had been undertaking high-altitude trials with a specially-designed monoplane called the Bristol Type 138A. To this day, Armstrong never knew why he had been selected; he could only assume that it was because as a graduate he had produced a widely-acclaimed paper on the effect of high-speed winds at altitude. Meteorology was a subject that had always fascinated him, and was a principal reason why he had applied to join the RAF as a pilot at a slightly older age than most; there, he could combine the thrill of flying with firsthand study of the elements. Commissioned in 1934 after passing through the Royal Air Force College, Cranwell, he had flown Bristol Bulldog biplane fighters for 18 months before his spell at Farnborough; in his absence the squadron had converted to Gloster Gauntlets, which he had also flown until the first Spitfires were delivered in 1938.

The Spitfire had been a joy, and the future had stretched ahead of him rosily, with prospects of early promotion to flight lieutenant and command of his own flight. Now there was this. He couldn't help wondering, not for the first time, what he had done wrong.

"We use this hut as an office block," Royston explained as they reached the building. "The accommodation is in the other one, and there's a shed behind the hangar we use as a canteen. But come along in, and I'll explain."

He opened the hut door and led Armstrong into a narrow corridor. There were rooms on either side, their doors closed. The corridor opened in to a larger room, with a table in the middle and some armchairs that looked somewhat the worse for wear. There was another door at the far end, and next to it a large map was pinned to the wall. It showed the British Isles, north-west Europe and part of the North Atlantic.

"Make yourself comfortable," Royston said, indicating an armchair. Armstrong shook off his damp trench coat and laid it on the table while Royston went to the other end of the room, opened the door and peered round its edge. He spoke to someone unseen, then returned and sat down opposite Armstrong, crossing his legs and taking a cigarette case from a pocket of his overall. He extended the case towards Armstrong, who shook his head.

Royston lit a cigarette, taking his time, and leaned

back in his chair with a sigh, watching the blue-grey smoke drift through a sunbeam that made a pool of light on the polished linoleum that covered the hut floor.

"Ever heard of a chap called General Baron Werner von Fritsch?" he asked suddenly. "No? Well, he's one of Germany's best. A cavalry officer of the old school, very astute. Some time ago, he let fall a prophetic remark. It was widely reported in military circles. 'The next war,' said old von F., 'will be won by the side with the most effective photographic reconnaissance.' And d'you know something, Armstrong? He's absolutely right. And that's why we're here. Welcome to No 1 Photographic Reconnaissance Flight."

He noticed Armstrong's raised eyebrows and grinned. "Don't get too excited, though. We aren't exactly well-equipped, at least not yet. We've been promised a couple of Spitfires, modified for high-altitude, long-range work and fitted with cameras, but it will be a while before we get them. In the meantime, we plan to use the Heinkel to take the occasional peep behind the curtain, so to speak. With a bit of luck it will fool the opposition. She's quite an interesting aircraft; we borrowed her from Rolls-Royce, who have been using her for engine trials. She's fitted with a specially supercharged Kestrel engine, and we can get her up to about 27,000 feet. Rolls-Royce weren't flying her around with a swastika plastered on her tail, of course; we added that when we took her over."

The Wing Commander's face took on a very

serious expression, and he leaned forward to gaze directly at Armstrong. "I don't have to tell you that we are going to have to fight Germany again, and probably very soon. The point is that we can't afford to wait until the shooting starts before we set about gathering the photographic intelligence we need."

Royston rose and went over to the wall map, beckoning Armstrong to follow him. He studied the map for a moment, then asked: "When war does come, where do you think the decisive battles will take place?"

"In the air, I should imagine, sir," Armstrong replied immediately. "The side that gains air superiority will also win the battle on the ground. It happened in Spain, after all."

Royston nodded. "Yes, it did. But in a major European war, involving Britain, this is where the real decision will be forced." He planted his index finger firmly in the middle of the North Atlantic.

"You may bet your bottom dollar," he said, "that when war does come the Germans will do their damndest to starve Britain into submission. We depend on our ocean lifelines, and we know that the Germans are gearing up for an all-out war on the high seas. There won't be a repetition of last time, when their fleet was penned up uselessly after the Battle of Jutland."

He took a long pull on his cigarette, looked around, and stubbed it out half-smoked in a convenient ashtray before continuing.

"They are building ocean-going submarines. They are building fast, modern, heavily-armed battleships and cruisers. There's even a rumour that they might build aircraft-carriers. Everything points to a determined effort to gain command of the seas. However" – he turned back to the map again – "whatever they do in naval terms is restricted by the simple fact of Germany's geographical position. Look."

Royston indicated a spot on the map on the north German coast. "To get out into the Atlantic from their main naval base here, at Wilhelmshaven, they have a choice of two routes. The first is through the English Channel, which would be so dangerous as to be out of the question once hostilities started; the second is here, through the gap between Scotland and Norway." His finger traced a north-westerly path past the Shetland Islands, the Faeroes and Iceland, then south-west through the narrow passage between Iceland and Greenland.

"The Denmark Strait," he said. "That's the way they'll go, you may depend upon it. And once they're out into the broad ocean they can lose themselves. They'll be out of air surveillance range and they can pop up at any point of their choosing, to knock hell out of our shipping. The Royal Navy would do its best to track them down, of course, but it would be like looking for a needle in a haystack."

He was interrupted by a knock on the door. He reached out to open it, and an extraordinary figure entered the room, carrying a tray on which rested a teapot, cups and saucers, milk, sugar and a plate of biscuits. The man who bore it seemed exceedingly old; he wore a pinstriped suit and a wing collar that only partly concealed a scrawny neck. He was completely bald and walked with a pronounced stoop, his hooked nose bobbing dangerously close to the teapot as he crossed the room to place the laden tray on the table.

"Thank you, Max," Royston said, smiling at the aged person. "This, by the way, is Mr Armstrong, who has just joined us. Max is our indispensable retainer," he added by way of explanation. Max turned to Armstrong and bowed slightly. Armstrong noticed that the man's eyes were a vivid blue, piercing and almost translucent, with none of the rheum normally associated with old age. He left the room without a word.

"More to him than meets the eye, too," Armstrong said, as Royston poured the tea. It was a statement, rather than a question. Royston grinned, rather secretively.

"You could say that. He has, shall we say, a number of attributes other than the making of tea. He is Lithuanian, and he is fluent in German. He also has a knowledge of certain codes and cyphers which are extremely useful in our work, but I'll say no more than that."

He handed Armstrong a cup and indicated the milk and sugar. "Help yourself. Speaking of our work, I had better tell you exactly what that is, and why you have been brought in. Remember your time at Farnborough? Well, we are going to need pilots with high-altitude experience, and you are one of the few who have been higher than 40,000 feet."

Armstrong remembered the experience very well indeed: the indigo of the sky, the curvature of the

Earth on the far horizon. From a height of seven and a half miles the familiar contours of the ground, covered with speckles of cloud, merged into a flat, brown monotone broken here and there by the glint of a river. The vista was hard to describe; you had to experience it.

On three occasions the Bristol 138A had taken Armstrong up to 42,000 feet, but there were others who had been even higher. In September 1936 a squadron leader called Swain went up to 49,967 feet, and just under a year later a Flight Lieutenant Adam took the Bristol to an incredible 53,937 feet.

The thing Armstrong remembered most about his own flights to high altitude in the Bristol was the bitter, paralyzing cold that had penetrated the special pressure suit designed by Siebe Gorman, the diving-suit firm, in collaboration with scientists at Farnborough. He also recalled the "dead man's handle" fitted to the control column; if the pressure suit failed and the pilot lost consciousness, his grip on the control column would relax and the device was supposed to close the throttle automatically, so that the Bristol would glide down to less hostile altitudes where it was hoped that the pilot would recover.

"We hope to have our first Spitfire by the middle of September," Royston said, breaking into the other's reminiscence. "In the meantime, we'll have to make do with the Heinkel. We won't be sticking our necks out to begin with – just taking a quick look at one or two naval objectives on the periphery to see what the Huns are up to. Our task is to detect any movement

– any movement at all – of the German fleet, and there's no doubt at all that it will begin to move to its war stations some time before any outbreak of hostilities.

"We are under Admiralty control, by the way, even though everyone here is RAF, apart from Max, of course, and one or two civilian specialists." He grinned. "It's a small firm at the moment, but it will grow. Our main concern is to avoid attention, which is why we picked this place; it's nicely out of the way and our cover is pretty good. So is our security, just in case you were tempted to think otherwise. There are people keeping an eye on things, although it wouldn't do to have guards pounding around everywhere, armed to the teeth. That would give the game away completely. The cat will be out of the bag when the Spitfires arrive, of course, but by that time I don't suppose it will matter."

Royston finished his tea and got up. "That's all for now," he said with a yawn. "I'm off for a wash and brush up. Come on – I'll show you where home is. We'll have another chat over dinner. Incidentally, it's civilian clothes at all times, until further notice. I'll show you round the Heinkel later on, and you can check out on her tomorrow. I can't tell you when we begin operational flying, for the simple reason I don't know. We just have to wait, and be ready."

At the hut doorway the Wing Commander stopped suddenly and turned to Armstrong. His expression was once again serious.

"Today is the sixteenth of August," he said. "It's

my guess that Hitler will move against Poland at the beginning of September, and perhaps even before this month is out. We are going to have a lot of work to do, and it won't be a piece of cake. The Hun ports are heavily defended. But make no mistake: a great many people are depending on us. All the risks are justified.

"And that," he concluded with a rather embarrassed smile as he walked out into the afternoon sunlight, "is probably the longest speech you'll ever hear me make."

Chapter Three

It was a beautiful morning. 5000 feet below the vibrating wings of the nine fighters the silver snake of the River Vistula wound its way through the September colours of the Polish countryside, finally disappearing under the thin curtain of haze that shimmered over the horizon.

The fighters, gull-winged PZL P-11Cs of the Polish Air Force, were fighting hard to gain altitude, their noses pointing towards the north-east. From the cockpit of his *Jedenastka*, as the little aircraft was affectionately known, Lieutenant Stanislaw Kalinski scanned the horizon over to the left; the treacherous quarter of the sky from which the formations of the *Luftwaffe* came to unload their deadly cargoes on Polish targets, their guardian Messerschmitts roving everywhere to challenge Poland's pitifully outclassed fighter defences.

Kalinski still found it hard to grasp that it was only a few hours since the first waves of *Stukas*, Heinkels and Dorniers had come sweeping out of the western sky without warning, pounding the forward Polish airfields, shattering military installations and blasting gaps for the armoured columns that were now spearing into his homeland. He was still dazed by the sudden fury of the German attack in the early hours of this black Friday, the first day of September 1939; both he and his fellow pilots had known that war was inevitable, but now it had come it seemed unreal.

Slightly ahead of Kalinski's aircraft and to the right, the *Jedenastka* flown by his squadron commander, Major Lesniewski, rose and fell gently on the warm currents of air, its red-and-white chequered insignia standing out boldly against its drab olive-green camouflage. It might have been just another pre-war training flight; at any moment now, thought Kalinski, they would emerge from the nightmare and return to base for a meal.

It was then that they saw the enemy: a cluster of black dots, sliding low over the Vistula away to port. Opening the throttle, Kalinski brought his P-11 alongside Lesniewski's aircraft and waggled his wings, pointing frantically at the enemy formation. The Squadron Commander waved in acknowledgement and winged over into a dive, followed by the other eight fighters. The wind screamed past Kalinski's open cockpit as the *Jedenastka* gathered speed, plummeting down towards what could now be clearly recognized as slim, twin-engined Dornier 17 bombers; there were seven of them, holding a tight arrowhead formation.

With eyes only for the leading bomber, Kalinski levelled out and sped towards it head-on, crouching low in the cockpit as tracers flickered past from the Dornier's nose-gun. The Pole forced himself to hold the fighter rock-steady as the distance between the two aircraft narrowed with terrifying speed, holding his fire until the bulk of the Dornier filled the sky ahead. A gentle pressure on the trigger, and a stream of bullets from the *Jedenastka's* twin 7.7 mm machine-guns tore into the enemy bomber at point-blank range. At the last moment, Kalinski rolled the little fighter over on its back and pulled on the stick, missing the Dornier's pale blue belly by inches. Completing his roll, he pulled the P-11 up into a steep climbing turn and looked back in time to see the Dornier nosedive into a field and erupt in a tremendous explosion as its bomb-load went off.

There was no time for jubilation. Pushing the throttle wide open, he came up behind a second Dornier, closing right in to 50 yards and firing in short, vicious bursts. Bullet strikes danced and sparkled over the bomber's dark green wings and fuselage. Suddenly, a jet of flame burst from the Dornier's starboard engine. Kalinski fired again, and this time the bomber's "glasshouse" cockpit shattered into fragments. The stricken aircraft went into a steep climb, hung poised for a moment, and then spun into the ground.

Climbing, Kalinski looked around. The remaining Dorniers had jettisoned their bombs and were heading flat out for the border. There was no sign of the other Polish fighters. Later, when he landed, Kalinski learned that the rest of the squadron had jumped a second formation of nine Dorniers, shooting down no fewer than five of them. With Kalinski's two, that made seven –

and all the Polish fighters had returned safely to base.

Nevertheless, their victory did little to boost the Polish pilots' morale. For every German aircraft they destroyed there seemed to be ten more to take its place, and each pilot was grimly aware that if the Dorniers had been escorted by Messerschmitts, the outdated P-11s would have been massacred. The Poles would go on fighting for as long as they had aircraft to fight with; but in his heart of hearts Kalinski knew that unless Britain and France came to Poland's aid immediately, the struggle was hopeless. Time, he realized with bitter certainty, was not on his country's side.

Armstrong awoke with a start. The night had been hot and he had slept with curtains and window open; a shaft of pale yellow sunlight made a square pattern on the wall next to his bed. He raised himself on an elbow and twisted his neck to peer at the clock on his bedside locker. It was five-thirty, and for a moment he toyed with the prospect of snatching another half-hour of sleep before his batman came along with the morning mug of tea. He knew that he certainly wouldn't be able to sleep after he had taken a sip of the stuff; you could clean brass buckles in it, stand spoons upright in it and poison rats with it. In fact, you could do just about anything you liked with it except drink it.

Dismissing thoughts of sleep, he threw aside the single sheet that covered him, swung his legs over the edge of the bed and pushed himself upright, raising his arms and stretching to his full extent on tiptoe. Naked, he crossed to the window and stuck out his head, inhaling the fresh morning air. Past the end of one of the hangars, he had a limited view eastwards over the airfield, to where the sun was rising through a thin band of mist. Its light was already powerful, and he narrowed his eyes against it.

Reaching a decision, he went to his locker, rummaged around on the bottom shelf and pulled out a folded singlet and pair of shorts, which he quickly pulled on. From under his bed he retrieved his track shoes, turning them over as he always did and inspecting them for signs of wear and tear. Shoes in hand, he left his room, paid a brief visit to the lavatory and headed along the corridor to the main door, which someone had left open during the night to admit air. Kneeling at the threshold, he donned his footwear and then stepped out into the morning, sniffing the now-familiar fragrance of the Suffolk countryside.

Rounding the front of the hangar, he walked a hundred yards to loosen his muscles and then broke into a jog, maintaining a leisurely pace for another couple of hundred yards along the edge of the airfield and then gradually speeding up until he was running comfortably at his best long-distance pace. The sun's warmth was not yet apparent and the air felt pleasantly cool on his skin.

He felt his body opening up to the challenge of running. He had always loved this form of lone exercise, when the only opponent was himself and he could push himself as much or as little as he liked. He had always been something of a loner as far as team games were concerned, and although he didn't mind participating in them he had never gone out of his way to cultivate them.

By the time he had completed a full circuit of the airfield he felt completely toned up and ready to face anything. He noticed that the buildings were gradually coming alive; there was a trickle of smoke from the cookhouse chimney and a couple of men in overalls were moving towards the principal hangar.

Walking the last hundred yards to cool down, he re-entered the accommodation hut and almost fell over his batman, a small cockney of indeterminate age called Smithson. Scrawny, and with close-set eyes peering past a huge hook of a nose, Smithson looked for all the world like a marabou stork. Armstrong had no idea whether the man was civilian or a serviceman. He saw that Smithson was clutching the dreaded mug of tea.

"Lor' love yer, sir," Smithson exclaimed, "I been lookin' for yer all over. Tea, sir?" He extended the mug, which steamed malevolently and gave off a smell like boot polish. Armstrong smiled weakly and took it.

"Thanks, Smithson. Just the job. I'll drink it after I've had a shower." Smithson looked unconvinced, but nodded anyway. "Oh, by the way, sir," he said as he handed over the mug, "the CO wants to see you as soon as possible."

People are up and about early today, Armstrong thought as he took his shower, and wondered what this early summons might mean. He tipped the tea into a washbasin, whose ingrained yellowish colour indicated that others followed the same ritual, shaved carefully and went back to his room to dress. Civilian clothes were still the order of the day and he put on a light cotton shirt, blazer and flannels, selecting an appropriate-looking striped tie to go with the ensemble.

Royston was not in the mess hut, and Armstrong eventually tracked him down in the operations room, leafing through a sheaf of signals. He nodded at Armstrong as the latter entered, then plucked a large spotted handkerchief from his breast pocket and blew his nose into it noisily. Armstrong noticed that the Wing Commander's eyes were red.

"Hay fever," Royston explained. "Bloody nuisance. The doc won't let me fly when it's bad; can't convince him that it clears away at altitude. Ah, well." He leaned back in his chair, arms folded, and gazed at Armstrong for a few seconds before continuing. His voice was very quiet.

"The balloon's finally gone up, Ken. Jerry has invaded Poland."

Armstrong had often wondered what he might feel when this moment came. Now he knew. It was an odd mixture of dread and elation. "Well, we've been expecting it. How long before we get involved, d'you think?"

Royston shook his head. "Don't really know. A couple of days, I suppose. There'll be a lot of diplomatic activity, an ultimatum of some sort, I expect. One thing I do know, though: Jerry won't back down. We ought to have gone for their throats at Munich. Bloody politicians." There was bitterness in his voice.

"What now, sir? As far as we are concerned?"

"There's a plan afoot to pool our resources, such as they are, with those of a rather peculiar outfit at Heston," Royston told him. Heston, Armstrong knew, was the commercial airfield in Middlesex from where many airlines operated services to the continent.

"What sort of outfit?" Armstrong wanted to know, as the Wing Commander paused to light a cigarette. Royston exhaled, coughed, and surveyed the cigarette with an expression akin to disgust. "I'm going to pack this in," he said, not altogether convincingly, and motioned to Armstrong to sit down in a chair opposite.

"Let me start at the beginning," he said. "There's a remarkable chap called Sidney Cotton. He's an Australian, and he was a pilot in the Royal Naval Air Service during the last war. He's been involved in all sorts of business ventures, most of which have combined flying and photography. He set up an air mail service in Newfoundland, did aerial survey work and started a commercial colour film company." Royston grinned suddenly. "Perhaps most important of all, at least for types like us, he invented the Sidcot flying suit."

Armstrong, like Royston, had used the warm, high-altitude suit on several occasions. "So that's where the name came from," he said. "I often wondered."

Royston nodded. "Yes. Well, early this year Cotton founded a little company in London called Aeronautical Research and Sales. Its backing came from the Air Ministry – unofficially, of course. It has an office in St James's Square and Cotton is its president and chief sales representative. He operates a Lockheed 12A – you know, the little American twin-engined airliner – out of Heston."

Armstrong, listening intently, wondered where all this was leading. The puzzlement must have shown on his face.

"I'm coming round to the important bit," Royston smiled. "The point is that for the past few months, Cotton has been flying all over Europe – including Germany and Italy – in the Lockheed, which incidentally is painted duck-egg green, on visits to aviation-related business concerns. He's even taken some of the German top brass for trips – including the air force boss, Hermann Goering, or so rumour has it."

Royston chortled, then blew his nose again. "Can you picture it? Old fatty Goering himself, enjoying a flight with the affable Sidney Cotton – and never dreaming that right under his feet, cleverly concealed from prying eyes by extremely tight-fitting port covers, were three F.24 cameras with five-inch lenses, positioned so that they could take left – and right-hand obliques and a vertical at the same time. They allow Cotton to photograph a strip of terrain eleven and a half miles wide from 20,000 feet, and there's a clever system whereby hot air is channelled over them to stop them from freezing at high altitude. The Lockheed has extra fuel tanks that increase its range to 1600 miles, and there's even method in the colour scheme; it makes the aircraft practically invisible from the ground."

Armstrong was full of admiration. "I'll be damned. Has he managed to get a fair amount of coverage?"

"Oh, yes. I've seen some of it. But here's the silly part: because we're run by the Admiralty, and Cotton's show is run by the Air Ministry, neither of us knew that the other existed until a few weeks ago. We've even been photographing the same bloody targets, including Wilhelmshaven. Still, I've had a few meetings with him since then, and our respective lords and masters think that we should pool our expertise, if that's the right word to use. Cotton thinks that stripped-down Spitfires are the answer too, by the way. With the Admiralty and Air Ministry apparently thinking along the same lines at long last, we might just get 'em a bit sooner.

"I hope so," he added thoughtfully, stubbing out his partly-smoked cigarette. "With what we've got, I've a feeling that our days are just about numbered."

He shrugged and stood up, stretching. "To hell with it. Sufficient unto the day, and all that. Let's go and grab some breakfast."

Chapter Four

For two weeks now, the German Fleet had been heading for the open sea. First the U-boats: 19 of them, slipping out from Wilhelmshaven to take up their war stations in the North Atlantic and North Sea, awaiting the inevitable.

Then the battleships: first the mighty *Admiral Graf Spee*, Captain Langsdorff's command, leaving Wilhelmshaven towards evening and using darkness to cover her passage through the North Sea so that she might slip into the Atlantic unobserved, there to join with her supply ship *Altmark* in readiness to fall on enemy shipping. Three days later her sister ship the *Deutschland* made a similar undetected passage, making for an Atlantic rendezvous with her own supply vessel, the *Westerwald*.

The ships of Germany's merchant fleet that were still on the high seas, in turn, were scurrying for their home ports or the harbours of neutral countries before the great grey warships of the Royal Navy had a chance to seize them on the declaration of war. For that was the aim of the British Government with the onset of war: the total blockade of Germany, enforced by the most powerful fleet in the world. And that meant, if possible, keeping the German warships that had not yet succeeded in slipping away to sea penned up in their harbours, where they could be attacked by RAF Bomber Command.

There was a problem. As the sun rose on this morning of Sunday, the third day of September 1939, the British Admiralty had no real idea how many German warships had put to sea, and how many remained in harbour. An open declaration of war on Germany might still be hours away, and a lot might happen in that time. When war came, RAF reconnaissance aircraft would legitimately be able to rove over the territory of the Reich; but the Admiralty needed vital intelligence now, intelligence that would enable the Navy's warships and the torpedo-bombers of the Fleet Air Arm and RAF Coastal Command to strike hard at the enemy's commerce raiders before they could inflict serious damage on Britain's ocean lifelines. And there was only one means of gathering that intelligence.

All this had been explained to Royston and Armstrong by a grim-faced Naval commodore when the two pilots had attended an Admiralty briefing on Saturday morning. And that was why Armstrong, a dawn later, was at 27,000 feet over the North Sea, flying the Heinkel 70 on what would almost certainly be its last clandestine mission, trying to avoid looking at the sun that rose bright and blood-red over the eastern horizon.

It was his first trip since the Nazis had invaded Poland, although Royston, still suffering cruelly from hay fever, had done one a couple of days ago – a sea search of the German Bight, looking for German battleships outward bound. He had not found any, because the battleships had already departed. Now Armstrong, his commanding officer grounded on doctor's orders, was on his way to make a final reconnaissance of Wilhelmshaven and its approaches – a mission which, he thought with misgivings, could only be described as extremely dangerous under the prevailing circumstances. He had an unpleasant gut feeling that this time the Germans would be waiting for him.

A few thousand feet below him clumps of fleecy fair-weather cumulus clouds drifted slowly by, casting their shadows on a dappled sea. They would provide welcome cover, should he need it.

He had worked out his flight plan carefully, in accordance with the briefing he had been given. The Admiralty wanted a great deal this time: not only pictures of Wilhelmshaven, but also of the Elbe Estuary, Cuxhaven, Bremerhaven, the airfield at Jever and the island of Wangerooge, where some curious installations had been spotted earlier.

His survival, he knew, depended on speed and surprise, particularly the latter. He planned to make landfall on the island of Sylt, off the coast of Schleswig-Holstein, then turn due south for the Elbe. He would turn over the bay, taking his photographs, then head in a direct south-westerly line for Wilhelmshaven, passing over Cuxhaven and Bremerhaven *en route*. A northerly turn over Wilhelmshaven would again take him in a straight line across Jever and Wangerooge and out to sea, his speed boosted by a forecast 30-knot southerly wind. Even if he was sighted, it was unlikely that the Germans would be suspicious of an aircraft flying along the coast in a westerly direction; but there was every chance that he would not be sighted, for the Heinkel had undergone a transformation. Taking a leaf out of Sidney Cotton's book, Royston had ordered it to be sprayed a uniform duck-egg green all over, so that it was virtually invisible at high altitude. The aircraft carried no national markings of any kind.

Despite the thick flying clothing he was wearing, including fleece-lined gloves and boots, Armstrong's hands and feet were numb. The sky five miles above the earth was a cold, inhospitable place; there would be some relief in the warmth of the sun as it climbed higher, but not much. The oxygen he was breathing was cold on his face, too; it came as a continuous supply through a crude, leaky cloth mask, and once the oxygen was turned on at 10,000 feet it continued flowing no matter whether the pilot was breathing in or out. It was a wasteful system, and Armstrong had already decided to make some recommendations so that the "boffins" could design a new and more efficient one.

He peered ahead through the early morning haze, checking his watch and gave a smile of satisfaction as the long strip of land that was Sylt appeared ahead, right on time. He held his course for another 30 seconds and then turned south, skirting the islands of Fohr, Pellworm and Nordstrand that flanked the coast of Schleswig. As he completed his turn, he looked back and was thankful to see that there was no white trail of vapour in his wake to betray his presence. Those trails, observed only recently as aircraft had regularly begun to fly above 25,000 feet, were still something of a mystery; some pilots thought that they were produced by the tips of the propellor blades, others – of whom he was one – that they were created as the hot gases from the engine froze in the upper atmosphere.

There was no time for speculation about that now. The Elbe Estuary was dead ahead and he flicked two switches, one to open the port that concealed his F24 camera and the other to set the film rolling. The magazine held 120 exposures, so with 6 targets to cover that meant 20 shots per target, at 15 second intervals. A counter near the camera switch told him how much film had been used up, so that he knew when to stop and restart the process.

Visibility was good, and there was no frosting on the cockpit canopy, inside or out. As he flew on, holding his course, he automatically rolled his head from side to side, scanning the sky on each quarter and occasionally checking below to make sure that there was no threat coming up from the danger area beneath the tail.

It was time to turn. He switched off the camera and swung the Heinkel's nose westwards, looking for the smoky sprawl of Cuxhaven, starting the camera again as the dark patch that was the port disappeared under his aircraft's long nose. After a five-minute run he altered course again, southwards this time, to take in Bremerhaven before curving to the west once more to cross Jade Bay and Wilhelmshaven. He found that he was breathing hard and sweating, despite the cold, as he calculated how much longer remained before he would be clear of these dangerous skies. The combination of cold and stress was producing an urge to urinate, but he had no means of relieving himself. Through experience, he knew that the pain would eventually give way to a dull ache, but the knowledge did nothing to lessen his present discomfort.

He was over Wilhelmshaven now, his camera working again as he flew north towards Jever. He was unable to locate the airfield's exact position, but he knew with fair accuracy where it ought to be and headed in that direction, trusting that the camera would register the necessary detail. All the while, he kept up his ceaseless quartering of the sky. There seemed to be no danger, but one could never tell, and he was at his most vulnerable while carrying out his dead-straight photographic runs.

He was almost over the coast now, with safety on the horizon, and he allowed himself to relax a little. It was a mistake. At that precise moment, his engine cut out.

For an instant, his ears having become attuned to the steady roar of the motor, his brain did not register the sudden silence. Then he saw the silver disc of the propeller break up into its component blades, windmilling slowly in the airflow, and a surge of panic hit him.

It did not last long. His mind, conditioned by thorough training, automatically took command and forced his hands and eyes into action, checking fuel, engine instruments and the mixture control that regulated the mix of petrol and air at altitude. Everything seemed to be in order; his tanks were still showing half full, there was no apparent loss of oil or coolant, and the mixture control was set correctly. There was nothing wrong at all – except that the engine had inexplicably ceased to function.

He trimmed the Heinkel for gliding at the best angle possible while he tried every trick in the book to restart the engine. Despite the aircraft's excellent gliding qualities he found that he was losing height rapidly as he crossed the coast. By the time he was over Wangerooge island he was down to 15,000 feet. Although there no longer seemed much point in photographing this final objective he reactivated the camera anyway, more as an instinctive gesture than anything else.

The altimeter showed 10,000 feet, and there was nothing ahead of him but open sea. There was no question of turning back towards Wangerooge in order to attempt a landing; the best he could hope for was to ditch the aircraft out to sea and trust that the water was too deep for the Germans to recover the camera and its incriminating film, assuming that they saw him go down. He knew that his own chances of survival were minimal; he had no lifejacket – just the inner tube of a car tyre, stowed away behind his seat. He was a mediocre swimmer; there was a faint possibility that the tide might cast him up on one of the islands off the Schleswig coast, in which case he might be able to reach Denmark, but he knew in his heart of hearts that the notion was little more than fantasy.

There was something niggling at the back of his mind, something to do with his present predicament. Suddenly it burst forth, like a flash of light, and he knew that he had been given one last desperate chance. He remembered the advice of his flying instructor, a veteran of the Great War. The words sounded in his head like the beat of a drum.

If your engine stops and all else fails, and if you have plenty of height, give her half throttle and do a steep dive to port.

Down to 6000 feet. There was time, but only just. Moving the throttle to the half-open position, he dropped the Heinkel's left wing and pointed its nose at the sea. The whine of the slipstream increased.

For a few heart-stopping seconds nothing happened. Then the propeller, which had become stationary during the glide, began to turn, slowly at first, as the pressure of the airflow built up against its blades. The speed of rotation increased and he held the dive, fighting an almost uncontrollable urge to pull out as the sea leaped up to meet him.

The engine gave a series of bangs and blue smoke belched back from the exhaust stubs. The propeller became a blur in front of his eyes and the Heinkel vibrated as the motor burst into full-throated life.

Keeping one hand on the throttle, Armstrong pulled back on the control column with the other, striving to keep the movement fluid. The force of gravity pushed him deep into his seat as the aircraft responded slowly – too slowly. The angle of the dive had lessened, but the sea still filled his windscreen. In desperation he let go of the throttle and placed both hands on the stick, hauling back with all his might. A reddish-grey veil obscured his vision.

When it cleared, the horizon was ahead of the nose and the sea was beneath him – about 20 feet beneath. Hastily, he put the aircraft into a shallow climb and turned on to a westerly heading, looking round dazedly. Off his left wingtip, the Friesian Islands were rapidly disappearing into the blue morning haze. The rising sun was high enough now to cast a shadow on the water ahead of his aircraft. It skipped over the wave crests, accompanied by a second shadow off to the right.

A second shadow! Armstrong's heart skipped several beats and he turned his head to look above and behind. He spotted the other aircraft at once, and the recognition posters that had adorned the crew room of his old Spitfire squadron flashed into his mind. He had studied this particular silhouette from all angles: shark-like fuselage with a low wing mounting two engines, twin fins, two crew – one a gunner in the rear cockpit, adding extra firepower to what was already a heavy forward-firing armament of two cannon and four machine-guns. It was a Messerschmitt 110 long-range fighter, and the Germans had given it a lot of publicity in their aviation magazines. They called it a Destroyer.

Armstrong held a steady course, trying to make his mind up what to do. The Messerschmitt was shadowing him, and so far making no attempt to attack. Armstrong decided to do nothing as long as the other pilot made no move, conscious that every mile was bringing him closer to safety. With the help of the tailwind he was doing over 200 miles per hour; he was already well clear of German territorial waters and a bit of mental dead reckoning told him that the English coast was about 55 minutes away.

He looked at the Messerschmitt again. It was falling behind, and he saw with dread that it was moving into a firing position astern of him, about 200 yards away. He knew that the pilot must have hesitated while he radioed for instructions, and that he had now been ordered to shoot the Heinkel down. Suddenly, Armstrong's fear left him and he became icily calm. He found himself putting himself into the German pilot's mind, could visualize with startling clarity his own aircraft centred in the 110's gunsight. He felt himself take a deep breath, just as the German must be doing as his finger hovered over the trigger, an instant before unleashing a storm of cannon and machine-gun fire.

To Armstrong, the next few moments would always be a blur, yet a blur in which everything seemed to happen in slow motion. Opening the throttle wide, he pulled the Heinkel into a steep right-handed turn, its wingtip pointing towards the sea. There was a hazy impression of the Messerschmitt flashing past, its nose lit up by vivid flashes, and of grey smoke trails spearing through the bit of sky which had been occupied by his aircraft only an instant ago. All this he glimpsed looking down through the cockpit canopy as the Heinkel rolled almost inverted, the Messerschmitt missing it by a matter of feet, spraying its gunfire uselessly into the sea in a welter of white foam.

The Heinkel was not exactly stressed for this kind of violent manoeuvring and Armstrong prayed that it would hold together as he continued the turn, pulling hard on the control column, until he was once more on his original heading. He levelled the wings as he headed for sea level in a shallow dive, looking for the Messerschmitt.

He saw it at once, a few hundred yards ahead, waggling its wings uncertainly in a reflection of the pilot's indecision as he tried to make up his mind which way to turn to begin another attack on his elusive quarry. He reached a decision at last and turned left, passing the Heinkel in the opposite direction prior to making a second attack from astern. As it did so, the 110's gunner opened fire, and Armstrong heard a series of sharp metallic bangs from somewhere behind him. There was no time to worry about that now; he was going to need all his concentration to stay alive.

Armstrong knew that the Heinkel, with its broad elliptical wing, was more manoeuvrable than the Me 110, and that its stalling speed was lower – much lower. He also knew that the German pilot would not be taken by surprise this time. When the Heinkel turned, he would slow down and follow it, seeking to bring his guns to bear.

Armstrong was banking on him doing exactly that.

He flung the Heinkel into another steep turn, this time to the left. The Messerschmitt pilot followed his action at once, as Armstrong had anticipated; most pilots turned left instinctively when taking evasive action, unless they happened to be left-handed, in which case they tended to turn in the other direction.

Slowly and carefully, at pains to make no abrupt movements, Armstrong began to tighten the turn. He had no need to look behind; he knew that the German pilot would be doing exactly the same, tied to the Heinkel by an invisible string as he strove to cut inside Armstrong's turn in order to bring his guns to bear. Armstrong also knew that the Me 110's gunner would not yet be able to traverse his machine-gun to a sufficient forward angle to take a shot.

He continued to tighten the turn, feeling the aircraft respond to the touch of his hand on the control column. It began to quiver slightly, and he knew that the next few seconds would be decisive. A few moments more, and the Heinkel would be on the verge of a stall – and at this height, only a few feet above the waves, there would be no chance of recovery.

Astern of him, and still off to one side, the Messerschmitt pilot swore out loud in rage and frustration as the steeply-turning Heinkel eluded his gun sight. The Messerschmitt began to shudder violently as it, too, approached its stalling speed. Still cursing, the pilot loosed off a despairing burst with his full forward armament of cannon and machine-guns.

The recoil was just enough to rob the Messerschmitt of the few vital knots of flying speed it needed if it was to stay in the air. Neither pilot nor gunner had more than a second or two to register terror before the Me 110 fell out of the sky, its downward-pointing port wingtip cleaving into the surface of the sea. The tail unit broke off with the violent impact as the fighter cartwheeled and remained floating on the surface as the rest of the aircraft plunged beneath, dragging its now unconscious crew with it.

Armstrong, narrowly avoiding the stall himself, levelled the Heinkel's wings and turned sharply to the right, looking back. He saw the spreading patch of foam and the floating debris and knew that he had won – this time.

Drenched in sweat, shaking and exhausted, he pointed the Heinkel's nose towards the western horizon, and home.

Chapter Five

I am speaking to you from the Cabinet Room at 10 Downing Street. This morning the British Ambassador in Berlin handed the German Government a final note stating that, unless we heard from them by eleven o'clock that they were prepared at once to withdraw their troops from Poland, a state of war would exist between us. I have to tell you now that no such undertaking has been received, and that consequently this country is at war with Germany . . .

Neville Chamberlain, British Prime Minister,
11.15 a.m., Sunday, 3 September 1939.

The Naval intelligence officers who examined the still-wet photographic plates developed from Armstrong's film could hardly believe their eyes. In the Schillig Roads, outside Wilhelmshaven's main harbour, lay a huge battleship, quickly identified as the *Admiral Scheer*, surrounded by an armada of light cruisers and destroyers. And that was not all: riding at anchor on the Elbe were the battle-cruisers *Scharnhorst* and *Gneisenau*.

Within the hour, sweating ground crews were

working flat out, loading armour-piercing bombs into the two squadrons of Blenheim bombers that had been standing by at RAF Wattisham since the news broke that the Germans had invaded Poland. The Blenheims' crews had been briefed to seek out German warships in the North Sea and attack them from high level, but now there were new orders: the warships would be bombed in their lair. Furthermore, the attack would have to be made at low level to escape the worst of the fire from the warships' heavy anti-aircraft guns, and armour-piercing bombs were no use unless they were dropped from a fairly high altitude.

So the cursing armourers had to start all over again and replace the armour-piercing bombs with ordinary 500-pounders, fitted with 11-second delayed-action fuzes. It was the fifth time the bomb loads had been changed in 24 hours.

At last everything was ready. Starting at four o'clock the ten Blenheims roared one by one down Wattisham's main runway and lifted away into an overcast afternoon sky. Led by Flight Lieutenant John Fairhurst, the most experienced pilot available, they sped over the Suffolk coast and set course eastwards, flying in two tight formations of five.

As the 10 Blenheims droned on, Fairhurst noticed that the cloud base was getting steadily lower. The sky was heavily overcast, forming a solid wall that extended up to 20,000 feet, and dark rainclouds scudded towards the German coast before a strong north-westerly wind. Soon, the Blenheims were flying in a narrow 300-foot gap between the cloud base and a heaving grey sea, the colour of slate. Sometimes, the aircraft were forced to fly as low as 50 feet.

Already, Fairhurst and the other pilots could feel the strain on their muscles. It was a nerve-racking, exhausting business, flying over the sea at this height. A false move would be fatal, and hitting the water at 200 mph would be about as soft as flying into a brick wall. But it was their only chance of finding the target.

Fairhurst peered ahead into the murk, running over the attack plan in his mind. At the briefing they had been told that the German pocket battleships were armed with only two types of anti-aircraft weapon, heavy guns and machine-guns, so the idea was to go in low where the heavy guns could not be brought to bear on them. They were to spread out and attack from three directions, to confuse the enemy gunners. The aim was to lodge the bombs in the ships' superstructures, where they would go off after a delay of eleven seconds. This meant that the pilots who made their bombing runs after the leader would have to go in with split-second timing, otherwise there was a very real danger that they might be blown sky-high by the explosions of the bombs dropped by the preceding aircraft.

The minutes went by, and Fairhurst glanced at the clock on his instrument panel. He calculated that the Friesian Islands were off to starboard, lost in the driving rain, with Heligoland up ahead. Right on cue, his navigator's voice crackled over the R/T. Fairhurst glanced down at him, hunched over his tiny chart table in the Blenheim's glazed nose. The third crew member, the gunner, sat halfway down the fuselage in his revolving turret, cut off from the others except for the intercom. With luck, the gunner would have little to do on this trip; the low cloud should keep enemy fighters at bay.

"Turning in 30 seconds, skipper. Stand by to turn on to one-three-oh degrees." There was no trace of nervousness in the navigator's voice; he was too intent on his task to notice the sea flashing past a few feet beneath him.

"Five . . . four . . . three . . . two . . . one . . . NOW!"

The Blenheim's starboard wingtip almost brushed the wavecrests as Fairhurst swung round on to the new heading, followed by the rest of the formation. The aircraft were now flying south-eastwards, directly towards their target. Rain streamed down the bombers' windscreens in rivulets. Once, a couple of trawlers flashed beneath their wings and were immediately swallowed up in the gloom behind them.

Suddenly there was land. An island slid by to starboard, and ahead was a coastline broken by a wide bay.

"Enemy coast ahead, skipper. That's the Jade estuary. We're right on target."

"Okay." The Blenheims roared on, heading straight for Wilhelmshaven. Amazingly, the weather began to clear a little. The rain stopped and the cloud base lifted perceptibly higher, to about 500 feet, which worried Fairhurst. Any further improvement in the weather would make them easy meat for the Messerschmitts.

Dead ahead, a long dark shape rose out of the water. It took Fairhurst's mind a moment to register the fact that he was looking at the *Admiral Scheer*, and that it was looming up with frightening speed. He flicked the R/T switch.

"Numbers four and five, break! All aircraft, make for the big one! Attack, attack!"

Led by Fairhurst, the first three Blenheims roared flat out towards the battleship. The other two aircraft broke to left and right and shot up into the clouds.

On board the Scheer, everything was normal. The sailors were going about their routine duties. From his lofty platform high up in the foremast, the flak control officer stared out across the grey water at the misty outlines of the neighbouring destroyers.

A sudden shout over the intercom jerked him into action. "Number four anti-aircraft position here, sir. Three aircraft bearing three-one-oh."

The officer raised his binoculars and scanned the sky off the warship's port bow. Three black dots were racing along just below the clouds, getting bigger every second. Twin engines, single fins. They looked like Junkers 88s. The officer swore. How often had those Luftwaffe idiots to be warned not to fly over the anchorage? One day, someone was going to give them a hot reception.

A yell from one of the lookouts on the platform shattered his thoughts. "Sir, those aren't ours! They're Blenheims! The Tommies are here!"

The strident blare of the alarm klaxon resounded

through the ship as the leading Blenheim closed in, thrumming steadily on above the waves. Hunched in the cockpit, Fairhurst doggedly held his course as the great battle wagon loomed up in front of him. He could see what looked like a line of washing strung across the after-deck. There was a hazy impression of white, upturned faces. Some of the sailors waved. Then they saw the red, white and blue roundels stamped on the Blenheim's wings and scattered in all directions.

"Bombs away!"

The navigator pressed the bomb release and Fairhurst hauled back on the control column. The warship's grey superstructure shot past, terrifyingly close. The two 500-pounders dropped away and curved down towards the *Scheer*. A shout came from the Blenheim's gunner. "Direct hit with one bomb – it went into the superstructure. I think the other bounced off the deck and went into the sea."

Damn, thought Fairhurst as he raced for safety, so low that the slipstream from the propellers fanned twin furrows on the surface of the water. Still, one hit was better than none at all.

"Watch out for the explosion," he ordered the gunner, mentally ticking off the seconds. He reached 15, and cursed aloud. A moment later, the gunner confirmed his suspicions.

"It hasn't gone off," the man shouted in disgust. "The bloody thing's a dud!"

The anti-aircraft gunners had woken up at last, and the *Scheer's* sombre hull twinkled with flashes as the ship's 20-millimetre twin-barrelled cannon –

the cannon that German pocket battleships were not supposed to have – sent streams of glowing shells after the twisting aircraft. The second Blenheim came in for its attack, racing through a wall of dirty black and yellow shell bursts. One of its bombs raised a thunderous fountain of water near the *Scheer's* side; the other, like Fairhurst's, failed to explode.

The dull sky was suddenly filled with brilliant light as the ships let fly with everything they had. Multi-coloured tracers arced up into the clouds from the barrels of more than 100 guns. Heavy batteries on the shore opened up with a vicious thud.

Midway through his attack run, the pilot of the third Blenheim suddenly pulled up into the clouds. He was obeying his instructions; he knew that he could not bomb within the 11-second time limit. Just before the swirling vapour swallowed his aircraft, he saw a blazing ball tumble out of the sky and plunge into the sea near Mellum Island. It was one of the diversionary Blenheims, caught in the meshes of the flak.

There was a momentary respite. The echoes died away and a haze of smoke drifted slowly over the water.

Then came a fresh alarm, as the five aircraft of the second flight came roaring in from the north-west. They ran smack into the combined fire of every gun in and around the anchorage. In the leading Blenheim, the pilot held his course automatically, mesmerized by the intensity of the enemy fire. Just like horizontal sleet, painted red, he thought.

It was his last thought. An instant later, a burst of

the glowing sleet smashed through the front of the cockpit, killing pilot and navigator instantly. More shells ripped into the fuel tanks, turning the aircraft into a blazing torch. Caught in a murderous crossfire from at least thirty 20-millimetres, the Blenheim disintegrated. One moment it was there, the next it had vanished. Burning fragments fell hissing into the sea from a spreading cloud of oily smoke.

The second Blenheim, streaming flame from both engines, crashed on the deck of the cruiser *Emden*, killing the first German sailors of the war. The third, dragging a long banner of grey smoke, climbed almost vertically towards the clouds, stalled and crashed near the shore. The fourth, bracketed by a cluster of heavy shells, cartwheeled over the water and subsided in a tangled heap of wreckage. The fifth somehow got through the barrage unscathed, dropped its bombs in a beautiful straddle across the *Scheer*, and vanished in the overcast. Again, the solitary bomb that hit the battleship failed to detonate.

As the surviving Blenheims droned away in the distance, a heavy silence fell over the bay. A cloud of smoke hung over the *Emden*, where a river of fuel from the crashed Blenheim's tanks still burned on the water.

Altogether, three bombs had hit the *Scheer*. Every one had been a dud. The attack had failed because of useless bombs; old bombs, stored too long in poor conditions. The price of failure had been 5 aircraft and 15 men.

On shore, a group of soldiers and civilians cautiously approached the wreckage of a Blenheim.

Pilot and navigator were trapped in the blazing debris, but the gunner had been thrown clear. A florid-faced civilian went up to the lifeless body and kicked it contemptuously. The next instant he was on his back, clutching a nose that poured blood. A young officer, a lieutenant, stood over him, his face white with fury.

"You bastard," he said, looking down at the grovelling man. "I should have you shot. These were gallant men."

The civilian struggled to sit upright and spat a clot of blood on to the ground as the officer turned his back on him. His eyes glittered with humiliation and hatred as he stared after the lieutenant. Upstart, he thought. I wonder how long that kind of chivalry will last?

Chapter Six

The Officers' Mess at RAF Fordingham, near Cambridge, was practically deserted. Armstrong had been on the station for a fortnight, his task to liaise with the crews of Bomber Command's specialist photo-reconnaissance squadron which was based here. It wasn't really an essential task, but Wing Commander Royston had decided that it was a good thing; in the absence of any aircraft to fly at Deanland, it would keep Armstrong occupied.

Armstrong now sported the two rings of a flight lieutenant on his sleeve; he had been back in uniform since the minute war broke out, and under the pilot's wings on his left breast he wore the blue-and-white ribbon of the Distinguished Flying Cross, awarded for his exploit over Wilhelmshaven. The immediate award of the decoration had come as a surprise to him, especially as his last mission in the Heinkel had been flown before the declaration of war. He knew that the second DFC of the war had gone to the chap who had led the raid on the enemy warships, a far more deserving case, in his eyes.

Morale at Fordingham was low, and small wonder. The reconnaissance squadron had lost three Blenheims in ten days; not one had returned with up-to-the-minute photographs of the German naval installations. People tended to drift into the bar, drink half a pint of beer without speaking to one another, and go to bed. It was the same at mealtimes; the aircrews sat at separate tables, avoiding one another's company as far as possible. The unspoken question hanging like a sword of Damocles over the Mess was: who is going to be next? The atmosphere was thick enough to be carved with a knife.

Amstrong was lounging in a leather easy chair in the mess anteroom, reading a tattered copy of *Punch* for want of anything better to do. He was the room's only occupant. Outside, the sun was setting; it was a glorious mid-September evening, and swallows twittered as they clustered in a long rank on a telephone line, ready to embark on the long flight that would take them to Africa for the winter. Armstrong envied them; at least they had a purpose. He had never felt so useless in his life. Every day, he prayed for a telephone call from Royston, telling him that the first of the promised PR Spitfires had arrived and recalling him to Deanland; so far, there had been nothing. So his days were spent in combing through intelligence reports of known or suspected German fleet movements, writing reports and assessments for the Blenheim reconnaissance squadron, and generally being ignored by the crews. It was not a happy situation to be in.

There was a polite cough, and he looked up to see one of the mess stewards hovering at his elbow. Armstrong raised an enquiring eyebrow.

"Would you like me to turn on the lights and

close the curtains, Sir?" the man asked. Armstrong nodded and took a last look out into the twilight.

"I suppose so, if you must. I was making the most of what was left of the day. The dark nights will be with us soon enough, and darker than usual, with the blackout."

"Very good, Sir." The man turned on the lamp beside Armstrong's chair and then methodically moved around the room, switching on the others and closing the heavy curtains. He departed softly, his footsteps making no sound on the carpet.

Wondering what to do with himself for the rest of the evening, Armstrong put aside his *Punch* and picked up a newspaper, turning to the radio programmes. An instalment of *The Four Feathers* followed by an orchestral concert was not a menu particularly to his taste. He sighed and stood up, stretching. Might as well head for the bar, he thought.

He went out into the corridor, turned left through the foyer, paused briefly in the cloakroom to retrieve his pipe and tobacco pouch from his raincoat pocket – the pipe was a habit he had acquired very recently, and he was only just learning to enjoy it – and continued through another short corridor to the bar's side entrance. The Officers' Mess was only three or four years old, having been built when the station was modernized as part of the RAF expansion schemes of the mid-1930s, and consequently the bar was well-appointed, with an L-shaped counter facing glass-topped tables surrounded by comfortable chairs.

Behind the bar, a mess waiter was polishing glasses. He wore a spotless white tunic with a high collar, and gold chevrons on his sleeve. His face brightened perceptibly as Armstrong came in.

"Evenin', Sir. What would you like to drink?"

"Oh, I think I could manage a pint, Corporal," the pilot said.

"Bit thin on the ground this evening, just for a change, eh?"

The corporal grinned ruefully as he pulled Armstrong's beer into a tankard, inspecting the result critically before he placed it on the bar top. "Been like this for a while now, Sir, as you've probably noticed. You're only the second person in so far."

Armstrong raised an eyebrow. "Oh? Who was the other one?"

"Officer over there, Sir," the waiter told him, inclining his head. Armstrong turned, and for the first time noticed a man sitting in a shadowy corner. Armstrong was about to invite the stranger to join him, but the other beat him to it. He rose and strolled to the bar, carrying a half-finished tankard of beer. As he came into the light Armstrong saw that he was a naval officer, a lieutenant. He was stocky, with square features and ginger hair. He came up to Armstrong and stuck out a hand.

"Thank the good Lord for a friendly face," he said, in an accent which – although refined by the King's English – failed to disguise an undertone that betrayed an origin somewhere among the Western

Isles of Scotland. "My name's Jim Baird, although everyone calls me Dickie."

"Glad to meet you, Dickie. Ken Armstrong. Can I top up that pot of yours?"

"There's no rush," the naval officer said mildly. "I can wait 'til yours is down a bit."

"That's easily arranged," Armstrong grinned, and downed his beer in one long swallow. He ordered two more pints, fished out his pipe and started to tamp tobacco into it, and then his curiosity overcame him. "What's a Navy type doing in a place like this?" he wanted to know.

"Somebody thought it might be a good idea for a Navy type, as you put it, to do a little tour of Bomber Command and teach the Air Force types the difference between Mr Hitler's ships and ours. There have been one or two – how shall I put it – unfortunate incidents. I drew the short straw. In the normal course of events I fly a thing called a Blackburn Skua, a sort of cross between a fighter and dive-bomber. I must admit that I'd rather be doing that than twiddling my thumbs in a dead-or-alive hole like this. Needs a damn good shake up, if you ask me."

Armstrong had already decided, even on a couple of minutes' acquaintance, that Lieutenant Baird was not afraid to speak his mind. He felt a little uncomfortable, having been brought up in an RAF school where "talking shop" in the mess was strictly taboo. He noticed that the barman, his back to them, was studiously pretending not to be listening.

"What about you?" Baird asked. "Are you

bomber, or recce?" As well as the reconnaissance squadron, Fordingham was home to two squadrons of Blenheim Mk IV bombers. At present they were absent, deployed elsewhere in the United Kingdom on some sort of exercise.

"Recce," Armstrong answered, "but not on Blenheims, thank God. Like you, I'm only visiting, so to speak." He did not elaborate. Baird glanced at his watch. "It's still early. What say we take a run ashore? I've got a car here, and I haven't had a chance to sample the local fleshpots yet."

Armstrong grinned at his companion's nautical turn of phrase. "Why not?" he concurred. "I should warn you, though, that there isn't much about in the way of flesh. I've done a couple of recces already. We could go into Cambridge, if you like. There's a decent pub called the The Blue Bells, with an equally decent blonde barmaid called Phyllis."

"I prefer the indecent ones, personally," Baird said. "Still, we'll have a look at it. Come on, drink up."

Baird's mode of transport was an Austin Seven. It looked as though it had made the acquaintance of more than one ditch, and Armstrong inspected it dubiously before he climbed in. "Are you quite certain this will go as far as Cambridge?" he asked, not altogether in jest.

"Don't worry about a thing," Baird said cheerfully. "It got me here all the way from Hatston, although admittedly part of the journey was on a ferry."

"Where's Hatston?" Armstrong wanted to know,

as Baird wrestled with the starting handle. His companion informed him that it was in the Orkney Islands. The Austin's engine coughed into life and Baird got into the driving seat, slamming the door behind him and moving off with a crunch of gears.

"Bloody awful place," he said. "Wall-to-wall mud. It's just been built. I was glad to escape for a bit. My squadron's going to be shore-based for a while; we flew in from *Courageous* a couple of weeks ago."

"What's it like, flying from a carrier?" Armstrong asked, trying to ignore the fact that Baird was negotiating sharp bends on two wheels.

"It's like everything else in life," the naval officer told him. "You get used to it. It has its hair-raising moments. I remember trying to land a Swordfish – that's our big torpedo-bomber biplane, as you may know – on the old *Furious* in the teeth of an 80-mile-an-hour gale; the bloody old Stringbag was actually flying backwards at one point."

Armstrong removed his unlit pipe from between his teeth; he was afraid that he might bite through the stem in his agitation as Baird careered on through the dusk. Luckily, it was not far to their destination, which was on the southern outskirts of Cambridge. A 15-minute drive found them within sight of the target, an attractive inn with white walls and a thatched roof. Baird brought the car to a stop immediately outside the open door and cut the engine; both men got out, Armstrong's legs feeling decidedly wobbly.

A single step at the threshold led straight into the public bar, a long room with oak timbers and a smoke-blackened ceiling. There was a broad hearth at one end of the room, with a fire laid in it but unlit; the weather was still pleasantly warm. It was Saturday evening, and little knots of men – farming folk for the most part, Armstrong knew – were seated at square, ancient tables, drinking and playing dominoes. A few of them looked up and nodded in friendly fashion as Armstrong and Baird entered; Baird attracted a few curious glances, for naval officers were something of a rarity in these parts.

Phyllis, as Armstrong had predicted, was behind the bar, furiously polishing glasses. She paused in her task and greeted the newcomers cheerily, addressing her opening words to Armstrong.

"Well, Sir, so here you are again. I see you've brought a chum along. That's nice." She thrust out an impressive chest in Baird's direction. "Royal Navy, eh? Bit off course, aren't you?" She giggled. Unlike most giggles, it was not an irritating sound.

"Two bitters, please, Phyllis," Armstrong said, reaching into his pocket for some change. As he did so, he felt a tap on the shoulder. He turned, and found himself gazing at the top of a bald head. Its owner was a small, plump man with a round face and watery blue eyes. He was in shirt sleeves, a waistcoat adorned with a massive silver watch chain stretched to bursting over his stomach. He wore pinstriped trousers and spats. He was sweating profusely, and dabbed at his forehead with a handkerchief. Armstrong thought that he caught a whiff of scent, and wrinkled his nose.

"Allow me to buy those drinks for you, gentlemen," the little man said. "It would be a privilege." He screwed a monocle into his right eye and peered at the medal ribbon on Armstrong's tunic. "Ah, the Distinguished Flying Cross, if I am not mistaken." His voice was high and piercing, and to Armstrong's discomfort it carried right across the room.

"Look," he said, "thanks for the offer, but we really couldn't. We're just having the odd one, and then we're on our way."

The little man was not to be put off. "Oh, but I insist," he squeaked. He pulled a crisp white five-pound note from his waistcoat pocket and laid it on the bar with a flourish. Some of the domino players at one of the nearer tables stared openly; to them, the fiver meant more than a week's wages.

Phyllis looked suspiciously at the plump man as she drew the beer. Looks like a sparrow with its tail pulled out, she thought.

The stranger ordered a large pink gin for himself and raised his glass to the two somewhat embarrassed officers before taking a sip. He volunteered the information that his name was Horace Wilmslow, and that he was a commercial traveller. He didn't say what his line was. Probably ladies' underwear, Armstrong thought uncharitably, or rubber goods, gentlemen for the use of.

"I travel all over the country," Wilmslow said with an air of self-importance. "Petrol rationing won't trouble me at all. Special allowance, you see, because of my line of business. Lot of government work, you know." He tapped the side of his nose, and peered at Armstrong's medal ribbon again.

"Being a man who keeps a close watch on the war news, it's my guess that you were awarded your decoration for the attack on Wilhelmshaven a couple of weeks ago," he said. "I can tell that it's new. Am I correct?"

Armstrong studied his beer. "Now," he said quietly, "you should realize that I can't talk about anything like that." He leaned forward suddenly and stared down at Wilmslow. "However, since you are obviously interested, I can tell you this much," he said in a conspiratorial whisper. "I got it for hunting gremlins."

In RAF slang, a gremlin was a mischievous, mythical creature held to be responsible for anything that went wrong. There were different sorts, explained Armstrong, all skilled in different kinds of evil. Orderly Room gremlins caused all the paperclips and drawing pins to vanish at the most awkward times; Watch Office gremlins tended to shoot off flares at the most inconvenient moments; Ablutions gremlins made sure that there was never any lavatory paper handy when it was most direly needed; and the flying gremlins were the worst of all. He looked at Baird, as though seeking confirmation.

"Ah, yes," the naval officer said with a completely straight face. "They're such a confounded nuisance that we must constantly remind ourselves about them by frequently reciting a simple ditty. It goes like this": Baird cleared his throat and adopted what could only be described as a theatrical stance.

"When you're seven miles up in the heavens
That's a hell of a lonely spot
And it's fifty degrees below zero
Which isn't exactly hot

It's then you will see the gremlins—
Green and gamboge and gold,
Male and female and neuter,
Gremlins both young and old.

White ones will waggle your wingtips
Male ones will muddle your maps
Green ones will guzzle your glycol
Females will flutter your flaps.

Pink ones will perch on your perspex
And dance pirouettes on your prop;
There's a spherical middle-aged gremlin
Who'll spin on your stick like a top!"

Armstrong, momentarily taken aback by Baird's unexpected poetic talent, quickly recovered himself. "There you are, then," he told the commercial traveller, whose mouth was hanging open. "Anyway, while up on this gremlin hunt, I got into trouble. There I was, upside down at 40,000 feet, with nothing on the clock but the maker's name— "

He was interrupted by a high-pitched, neighing laugh from Wilmslow. "I say, you fellows, you're having me on, aren't you? Never mind, I can take a joke. That's worth another round of drinks. Barmaid! Same again." He waved an imperious hand towards Phyllis, who ignored him completely.

"No thanks, really," Armstrong said. "We've got to take it easy."

"Ah, I see," Wilslow said, tapping the side of his nose again. "Flying tomorrow, I expect." He turned to Baird. "But what about you, er – Lieutenant, isn't it? What brings you to these parts? Is your home here?"

"Just visiting," Baird said curtly.

Wilmslow shook his head sadly. "This terrible war. It separates so many people. I do hope it will be over by Christmas, as many believe. It is all so unnecessary."

Armstrong and Baird stared at him. Armstrong felt his hackles beginning to rise. He set his glass down on the bar. "Unnecessary?"

"Of course. All Herr Hitler has attempted to do is restore his country to a leading position in Europe, to break free of the shackles imposed upon it by the shameful Treaty of Versailles. Look at his achievements in just a few short years – the industry he has created, the discipline, the pride. He has made Germany a bulwark against communism. That bulwark could be even stronger, if only our politicians had the sense to throw in their lot with him. That's what Sir Oswald Mosely wanted, but his aspirations were thwarted by a conspiracy between the communists and Jews."

Armstrong recalled the pitched street battles fought in the 1930s between the black-shirted members of Mosely's British Union of Fascists and their opponents – not all of whom, he knew, were communists.

"Haven't they just locked him up?" he queried mildly.

"A tragedy!" Wilmslow huffed. "A terrible tragedy for this country! Such a great leader. Such wasted talent."

Armstrong was suddenly conscious of another presence. He halfturned to face another man, one of the domino players, who had quietly approached the bar. He was a big fellow, a good six feet four inches tall, deeply tanned by years of exposure to the elements. He wore corduroy trousers and what appeared to be a moleskin waistcoat over a rough, striped shirt. He had hands like shovels. He grinned amiably at Baird and Armstrong.

"Just mind your backs a minute, lads, if you don't mind."

The two officers stepped aside hurriedly, eyeing the massive hands. The farmer – for such he was – reached down, seized the commercial traveller under the armpits and, with no apparent effort, lifted him off the floor like a sack of potatoes. Slowly, he raised him until Wilmslow's eyes were on a level with his own. The farmer gave a grin that would have done justice to a timber wolf.

"I think," he said in a low rumble, "that you had better bugger off." Wilmslow made a strangled bleating noise and turned scarlet. He began to slobber at the mouth.

"Come on now, Jed Cartwright," Phyllis said sharply, "he'll be having a fit if you're not careful. If you must do him in, take him outside first."

"Aye, all right, Phyllis. Open the door, Barney, will you?"

A little man with a wizened face and a battered trilby hat perched on the back of his head got up and did as he was asked, grinning broadly. He gave a mocking bow as Jed crossed the room, still carrying the squirming Wilmslow, who was now twittering about having the law on all and sundry. Jed whispered something in his ear, and the twittering ceased. The two disappeared outside. An expectant hush fell over the bar. From outside there came a distinct thud, closely followed by a squeal, as Jed's boot came into violent contact with Wilmslow's backside. The farmer came back indoors and sat down at his table.

"Not standin' for that sort of talk," he said. "Bloody Germans." He picked up his hand of dominoes and glared at his fellow players. "I hope nobody's been havin' a peek at these while I was busy," he said menacingly.

Baird looked at his companion and raised an eyebrow. "Well, that's removed a rather nasty smell," he said. He looked at the drinks Wilmslow had forced on them and pushed them across the bar. "I think those would choke us now, Phyllis. Two more, please."

"On the house, Sir," the barmaid said, fluttering her eyelashes at him. Armstrong chuckled. "Looks as though you've clicked. I knew I wouldn't have a snowball's chance in hell the moment the fleet moved in."

Baird's face was serious. "I hope to God there

aren't many like him," he said, referring to the humiliated Wilmslow.

"Im afraid there probably are," Armstrong told him. He grinned and glanced at Jed, engrossed in his dominoes. "I reckon they're outnumbered, though," he added.

The pilot's gaze travelled around the room, taking in the little knots of men as they relaxed after their day's toil. The harvest was in, and they were contented. He suddenly realized that he was witnessing a tableau that typified the British way of life as it had been for centuries, a comfortable, orderly pattern that was now in dire peril of being destroyed forever. This will not be over by Christmas, he thought. It will be a long, hard and bloody battle, and God only knew what the world would be like when it was over.

INTERLUDE: POLAND

A thousand miles from where Armstrong and Baird were drinking their beer, Stanislaw Kalinski and his fellow pilots – pitifully few of them were left now – had already had a bitter vision of that future world. They had seen it in the blazing ruins of Poland's ancient and beautiful cities, in the corpses strewn by the roadsides, in the smoking wreckage of aircraft plunging to earth.

Kalinski knew that there was no shame, for he and his peers had battled on valiantly to the bitter end, holding on while they awaited reinforcements in the shape of Hawker Hurricane fighters from England – reinforcements that never came.

In the first week of September, the Polish Pursuit Brigade, fighting in the skies over Warsaw, destroyed 42 enemy aircraft for the loss of 37 of its own. The cost was fairly equal in numerical terms, but the difference was this: whereas the Germans could replace their combat aircraft, the Poles could not. On 7 September, the remains of the Brigade were withdrawn from the Warsaw area to be reorganized. They never returned to the defence of the capital. Crippled by the lack of essential supplies and spares, the Brigade ceased to exist as an effective fighting force.

The turning point of the Polish campaign came on 8 September. On that day, several Polish divisions were surrounded near Radom and shattered by concentrated *Stuka* attacks, and the 4th *Panzer* Division reached the defensive perimeter around Warsaw. In the air the Polish position was desperate, with more and more aircraft being put out of action by the lack of spare parts and shortage of fuel. Only the Bomber Brigade was still able to operate in any strength, because its main supply base at Deblin was still functioning, but even so the bombers had suffered crippling losses, and their last major mission against enemy armour and supply columns was flown on 12 September. Scattered attacks were made after that date by aircraft operating in twos and threes, but they were of little significance.

Then, on 17 September, there came a new development: nine Soviet fighter-bombers swept down on a Polish airfield at Buczacz, strafing installations and the handful of aircraft that were left. In accordance with a secret agreement between Germany and the Soviet Union – an agreement that involved the partition of Poland between the two powers – Russian troops and armour came flooding into the country from the east.

For the Poles, it was the final, bitter stab in the back, but there was one last act still to be played in the Polish tragedy. On four occasions, between 18 and 24 September, *Luftwaffe* aircraft dropped leaflets over Warsaw, calling on the strongly-fortified Polish garrison to surrender. The Poles did not reply; instead, the 100,000 troops in the besieged city dug themselves in even deeper and grimly awaited the onslaught.

It was not long in coming. At eight o'clock in the morning of 25 September, wave after wave of bombers and dive-bombers droned over the city, systematically bombing it from end to end. By noon an immense pall of smoke hung over the Polish capital, rising to a height of 10,000 feet and spreading out in a great banner across the countryside. And the assault continued; for hour after hour, 400 bombers of *Luftflotten* 1 and 2 dropped 500 tons of high explosive on the city, pounding street after street into smoking rubble.

Early the following morning, stunned by the ferocity of the attacks, the garrison and what remained of the civilian population crawled out of their shelters and stared uncomprehendingly at the devastation around them. They knew that it was futile to resist any longer. That same day, the garrison offered to surrender, and the capitulation was signed on the 27.

It was hopeless to fight on. And yet . . . two hours before the victorious German troops marched into Warsaw, a trio of ancient R.31 army co-operation biplanes took off from Mokotow airfield, virtually under the noses of the advancing enemy, and machine-gunned a German convoy that was approaching the city. There was only time left for one pass before the Messerschmitts pounced. Seconds later, three funeral pyres blazed by the roadside.

Just before the end, what was left of the Polish Air Force – 54 bombers and 38 fighters, many of them damaged and barely airworthy – flew to neighbouring Romania. With them went Stanislaw Kalinski and the two surviving pilots of his squadron. They had no idea, as yet, what their ultimate destination might be; it didn't matter, as long as they could continue the fight.

They had lost a battle, and the experiences of the last few weeks had turned them into hardened, bitter men whose hearts were filled with an implacable hatred. But Poland's destiny, they told themselves, could wait. There was still a war to be fought.

Chapter Seven

Monday, 16 October 1939: 12.15 hours

The nine Junkers Ju 88 dive-bombers flew in two loose arrowhead formations, scudding between banks of cloud. An hour and a quarter earlier they had taken off from their base at Westerland, on the Friesian island of Sylt; below them now was the Firth of Forth. In the leading aircraft, the raid commander, *Hauptmann* Helmuth Pohle, could almost taste the rising tension as their objective crept nearer. Pohle's orders were to attack any warships sighted at the British naval base of Rosyth; at last, six weeks after the outbreak of war, German bombers were to venture into British airspace for the first time.

Pohle was conscious that the German Navy had beaten the *Luftwaffe* to first place in striking a telling blow; two days earlier, a U-boat commander called Gunther Prien had crept daringly into Scapa Flow in the Orkneys in the U-47 and sunk the battleship *Royal Oak* with heavy loss of life. A few hours later, reconnaissance aircraft, keeping a close watch on the east coast of Scotland, reported that the battle-cruiser HMS *Hood* had entered the Firth of Forth and appeared to be making for the anchorage at Rosyth. She was Pohle's principal target.

Pohle was content to fly in loose battle formation, for German Intelligence had indicated that the RAF had only a handful of obsolescent Gloster Gladiator fighters in Scotland. In fact, Intelligence was wrong. Fighter Command had two squadrons of Spitfires based near Edinburgh, and that very morning a squadron of Hurricanes had flown in to the airfield of Drem on the southern bank of the Firth.

Pohle's formation droned on. From 13,000 feet, the crews could see the sprawling, smoke-shrouded complex of Edinburgh, then the spidery structure of the Forth Bridge, beneath their wings. And there, dead ahead on the north bank, was Rosyth.

The first ship that Pohle saw in the harbour was the *Hood*, dwarfing the lesser warships that clustered around her. She presented a beautiful target. Pohle ground his teeth in frustration; on the personal orders of Adolf Hitler, the Ju 88 crews were not to attack the battle-cruiser if she had already entered harbour. At this stage of the war, both the *Luftwaffe* and the Royal Air Force had an unspoken, unwritten agreement that bombs were not to be dropped if there was danger of causing civilian casualties.

But there were several other cruisers and some destroyers anchored in the Firth and Pohle selected one of the former as his target, pushing the Junkers into a dive. Anti-aircraft fire was coming up in streams, exploding with a horrible gritty crunch, rocking the aircraft with near misses. Pohle fought to hold the Junkers steady as it screamed downhill in a 70-degree dive.

Suddenly, there was a loud bang and a gale of icy air roared into the cockpit. Pohle glanced up: the transparent escape hatch in the cockpit roof had gone. Desperately, he forced his attention back to the target, which now filled his sights. A second later, his bombs fell away and he was rocketing skywards again, crushed down into his seat by the g-force. One of the bombs exploded in the water; the other hit the cruiser HMS *Southampton* starboard amidships, smashed through three decks, emerged from the side of the hull and reduced the Admiral's barge, lying alongside, to matchwood. It failed to explode.

"*Achtung*! Enemy fighters astern, closing!" The rear gunner's voice was high-pitched with fear as he crouched behind his gun, watching the fighters as they bored in, steeling himself to hold his fire until they were within range.

They were the Spitfires of No 603 Squadron. Smoky lines of tracer from the Junkers' rear gun position flickered past the leading fighter's wings. The pilot braced himself and jabbed his thumb down on the firing button, seeing the strikes of his bullets dancing and sparkling on the Ju 88's dark green camouflage. There was a flicker of fire from one engine and the Junkers started to go down, two more Spitfires attacking it in turn.

Pohle's cockpit was a shambles. Engineer and rear gunner were both dead, and the navigator was lying on the cockpit floor in a pool of blood, retching and choking, a bullet through one of his lungs. Pohle spotted a trawler and turned towards it, using all his strength to keep the crippled aircraft flying on one engine. Then the Junkers ploughed into the sea with a jarring crash and he lost consciousness. A few minutes later the trawler crew fished him out of the sinking aircraft. He woke up five days later in Port Edwards hospital, with the sickening knowledge that his war was over.

It was a damp, depressing day, with a light drizzle sweeping in from the North Sea. The dampness glistened on the wings of the Vickers Wellington bombers, standing like forlorn cattle in their dispersals around Newton Heath airfield.

An armed sentry stood outside the main door of the Operations Block. The man, in dripping gas cape and steel helmet, brought his rifle to the slope and slapped its butt in salute as an officer approached. Armstrong returned the salute, showed the sentry his pass and went inside, shaking drops from his raincoat as he went. The depressing day matched his mood, for he was still leading the life of an itinerant, moving from bomber base to bomber base to carry out liaison duties. There was still no sign of the promised PR Spitfires, and such photographic reconnaissance as there was remained in the hands of the luckless Blenheims, which were still suffering appalling losses.

Back at Fordingham in September, Armstrong and Baird had decided that they would do their best to team up as they travelled around the bomber bases of East Anglia, and had put in the appropriate request to their respective authorities. There had been no objection; it seemed that nobody gave two hoots what they did. So here they were at Newton Heath, just up the road from Newmarket. The aerodrome was home to a single squadron of 12 Wellingtons, part of Bomber Command's No 3 Group, and in contrast to Fordingham, Armstrong and Baird had found the crews friendly and, for the most part, eager to assimilate the information the two officers were there to impart.

The bomber crews were itching to attack something, but the shipping searches they had been carrying out since the war started had proved fruitless. Armstrong had flown on a couple of them, and had seen nothing but grey seas and a few fishing boats. So far, the Wellingtons had suffered no losses due to enemy action – unlike the Handley Page Hampdens of No 5 Group. At the end of September, a formation of five aircraft had encountered enemy fighters off Heligoland and the whole lot had been shot down, information that had been gleefully passed on by a German radio broadcaster.

The telephone call that had summoned Armstrong to the Operations Block had come from the Senior Intelligence Officer, and Armstrong made straight for his office. He knocked, opened the door without waiting, and went inside. To his surprise, the Station Commander was present, seated at the SIO's desk; so was the Wing Commander (Flying), Dickie Baird and the SIO himself. Armstrong came to attention and saluted the Station Commander, Group Captain

Harrington. As he did so, he glanced at Baird out of the corner of his eye; his friend did not appear to be over-happy.

"Sit down, Armstrong," Harrington said, waving a hand towards a vacant chair. The Group Captain was a small man with greying hair and a chestful of medal ribbons; he had flown Sopwith Camels in the last war. Armstrong removed his cap and did as he was told, looking at the Station Commander expectantly.

"I'll come straight to the point," Harrington said. "You know that the Huns attacked Rosyth yesterday?"

Armstrong nodded. "Yes, Sir. I've seen the preliminary report. I understand they didn't do much damage, and that we got a couple."

"That's right. Well, apparently some politicians are making a lot of noise about the raid, and there's considerable pressure on the War Cabinet to take some sort of retaliatory action. The upshot is that the Chief of the Air Staff wants Bomber Command to carry out an attack on Wilhelmshaven. Not the town itself, of course, but on enemy shipping in the vicinity. Apparently the Huns used only a single squadron for the Rosyth raid, so we've been told to do something similar. When I say 'we' I mean the Wellington squadron here. Our name came out of the hat."

Harrington paused and cleared his throat. "The thing is," he continued, "I'd like you and Lieutenant Baird to go along as observers. Baird tells me that he's made an extensive study of Wilhelmshaven's layout, and you have actually been there, so you'll know what to look for. Any questions so far?"

Armstrong looked dubious. "I'm afraid I've very little night flying experience, Sir. I don't mind going, but I doubt that I shall be able to contribute anything useful in the way of observation."

Harrington shifted in his seat and picked up a pencil from the desk top, toying with it.

"Ah, well, you see, that's the other thing. Night flying doesn't come into it. We've been ordered to make a daylight attack, for fear of damaging civilian property."

Armstrong shot bolt upright in his seat, aghast. "But that's bloody well ridiculous!" he burst out. "I'm sorry, Sir, but Wilhelmshaven's a hornets' nest. I was almost clobbered there myself, and not one of the recce Blenheims sent out there has come back. Without fighter escort – and we've nothing capable of getting there and back – a daylight attack would be suicide."

"That's not what Wing Commander Goodison thinks," Harrington said, turning to the man who was seated next to Baird. "Over to you, Charles."

Armstrong did not like Goodison, who had a prim, haughty manner about him. The comments the Wing Commander made now did nothing to change his opinion of the man.

"Contrary to what you may think, Armstrong," Goodison said, placing emphasis on the "you", "the squadron has a very good chance of survival indeed. A squadron of 12 Wellingtons has very good defensive firepower: 72 machine-guns, to be precise. More than a match for any attacking fighters."

Armstrong was aware that each Wellington carried a pair of 0.303 machine-guns in the nose and tail turrets, and two more in beam positions in the fuselage. He also knew that the rifle-calibre guns were outranged by the cannon used by German fighters. And there was another deficiency. The Wellington was not fitted with self-sealing fuel tanks – in other words, tanks equipped with a rubberized lining that would close around any bullet hole and prevent fuel from escaping. He chose to make no comment about that.

"I am quite confident," Goodison went on, "that the squadron will get through to the target, complete its mission and fight its way out if necessary, and as far as I am concerned the matter ends there. Of course," he added, "no one is ordering you to fly on this mission, Armstrong. If you go, it will be strictly as a volunteer."

Armstrong, with a supreme effort of willpower, forced his anger to remain below the surface. "I have never indicated that I was unwilling to go," he said quietly. "It's just that I don't like going into a situation without knowing the odds."

"That goes for me, too," Baird said. Behind the desk, Harrington nodded approvingly. "Very well, gentlemen. That's that, then. The raid is scheduled for tomorrow morning; the weather will have improved by then, or so I'm assured. Take-off will be at 08.00, briefing at six."

"I thought for one dreadful moment that you

were going to thump the Wingco," Baird said to Armstrong a little later, as they walked away from the building.

"I felt like it," his companion said grimly. "Pompous ass. One thing's for certain – I'm not going to fly with the bastard tomorrow."

As things turned out, that particular problem did not arise. When they turned up for the briefing the next day, Armstrong and Baird found that they had been assigned to different crews. Armstrong's pilot, a flying officer, was a cheerful, ruddy-faced man with a New Zealand accent; his name was Pittaway and he had joined the RAF in 1937, having sidestepped all sorts of red tape in his own country after being rejected for pilot training in the Royal New Zealand Air Force. "Bloody old school tie rules the roost out there, I'll tell you," he confided. "Still, there are a lot of blokes like me who are mad keen to get into this war, and nothing's going to stop 'em, even if they have to swim here."

Pittaway's personality was reflected in the mood of his crew. There were five of them: observer, wireless operator, bomb aimer, nose gunner and rear gunner. They greeted Armstrong affably, those who smoked standing clear of the Wellington to savour a final cigarette while Pittaway walked round the big aircraft, methodically carrying out his pre-flight checks. The ground crew stood off to one side, talking quietly, waiting.

Armstrong had never been so close to a Wellington before, and was impressed by the aircraft's size. Its wings spanned nearly 90 feet from tip to tip and its fuselage was square and solid. Armstrong knew that the aircraft was extremely robust, thanks to its lattice-type construction: geodetic, they called it, or something like that. He had very briefly met the Wellington's designer during his time at Farnborough; a somewhat eccentric professor-type called Wallis, who had also designed the R.100 airship.

Having satisfied himself that the control surfaces were all in one piece, Pittaway checked with the armourer that the bomb load was correctly stowed, with the fitter and rigger that the aircraft was technically sound, and then signed the technical log, the Form 700, formally accepting the charge of the bomber from the ground crew. If anything went wrong now it would be his fault, not theirs.

Minutes later, the aerodrome thundered with sound as 24 powerful Bristol Pegasus engines coughed into life, roared briefly as pilots carried out their engine checks – confirming what the ground crews had already done some time earlier – and then settled back to a steady mutter as the throttles were closed again. Every crew member was conscious that their aircraft was heavily laden with fuel and 4,000 pounds of bombs – eight 500-pounders – and that the take-off run would be a long one. Any sudden loss of power in either engine at the critical point when the bomber was becoming airborne would spell disaster.

Pittaway's eyes were on the flying control caravan at the far end of the airfield. Suddenly, a white flare arced up from it. A few moments later

Wing Commander Goodison's aircraft began to move, waddling across the grass to the threshold of the airstrip. Two more followed it, then Pittaway signalled to his ground crew to pull away the chocks. They saluted to show that all was clear and the pilot opened the throttles. The Wellington vibrated and shuddered and then it too began to move, joining the queue.

Another flare went up from the caravan and Armstrong, watching through the perspex windscreen, saw Goodison's aircraft begin to gather speed on the grass runway. Its tail came up and then it was airborne, in a shorter distance than Armstrong had expected, daylight showing between its undercarriage and the airfield boundary as it climbed away.

A few minutes later it was their own turn. Pittaway's voice sounded over the intercom.

"Okay, everyone, here we go. Stand by for take-off. Second pilot, you have the throttles."

"I have the throttles," confirmed Armstrong, who was sitting alongside Pittaway in the second pilot's seat. The position would normally be occupied for take-off by the observer, who doubled up as second pilot when required. Armstrong placed his hand firmly on the throttle levers, leaving the pilot free to grasp the control wheel with both hands.

"Full power!" Pittaway ordered. The Wellington shuddered again as Armstrong carefully advanced the levers and the engines roared in response to his touch.

"Brakes off!"

Reluctantly, the laden aircraft began to move. Armstrong continued to hold the throttle levers firmly forward against the stops, concentrating on nothing else. Suddenly, he could see the runway ahead beyond the nose as the tail rose. For what seemed an age the bomber clung to the ground, the undercarriage rumbling, then it bounced two or three times and the rumbling ceased.

Pittaway applied the brakes to stop the wheels rotating and pulled up the undercarriage, letting the flying speed build up before entering a climbing turn, following the bombers that had already taken off. "All right," he said to Armstrong, "you can relax. I've got her. Enjoy the ride."

Armstrong relinquished his control of the throttles and sat back in his seat, looking out at the scenery as the Wellington climbed out over the Suffolk countryside that was so familiar to him. There was tranquillity there, and he felt reluctant to be leaving it; but strangely enough he felt no apprehension. He put that down to the fact that he had been to Wilhelmshaven before, and knew what to expect.

Over the coast, the Wellingtons formed up into three flights of four, then set course over the North Sea, levelling out at 13,000 feet. Ahead of them, the sky was almost cloudless.

It was completely cloudless over the island of Wangerooge, where the experimental *Freya* radar station kept watch up to a point 50 miles out over the North Sea. In recent weeks, a second, similar station had also been brought into service on Heligoland.

Seated before the flickering cathode ray tubes of the Wangerooge station, *Feldwebel* Walther Heide had not been on duty long enough to be bored. That would come later, when he had nothing to do but report the movements of occasional friendly aircraft such as the Heinkel He 115 and Dornier Do 18 seaplanes flying to and from their base at Norderney. It came as a considerable surprise, then, when both his screens – one registering range, the other azimuth – showed distinct traces. He stared at them for several seconds before he realized that the radar echoes were being returned to the station not by a single aircraft, but by several, flying in tight formation. What was more, Heide knew that this was not a *Luftwaffe* formation, returning from an armed reconnaissance over the North Sea; the Wangerooge and Heligoland stations were alerted to all such movements.

Heide pressed a buzzer at the side of his console and, after a short delay, an officer entered the room, a sheaf of papers in his hand and a look of annoyance on his face.

"Yes, Heide? What is it? Don't you know I'm busy?"

"My apologies," Heide said, "but I thought the *Herr Leutnant* should see this."

Frowning, the lieutenant peered over the NCO's shoulder and studied the traces for a while. "Well, Heide," he said at length, "what do you make of it?" Heide took a deep breath.

"I think, *Herr Leutnant*, that we are picking up an incoming bomber formation. Not ours, for certain," he added.

The officer frowned again. "The Tommies? In broad daylight and a cloudless sky? Even they wouldn't be that stupid." He looked at the display, which he could read as expertly as Heide. "Range 40 kilometres, altitude 4000 metres, bearing three-five zero . . . Looks as though they're making for Heligoland, whoever they are."

At that moment the Heligoland station came on the line, confirming that it was also tracking the incoming formation. The lieutenant shook his head, then reached for a telephone.

"We may be making fools of ourselves, Heide, but I'm not about to take any chances. Hello? Jever control, this is *Freya*. We are tracking what appears to be an incoming enemy formation, range now 30 kilometres, altitude 4000, bearing three five-five. Predicted target Heligoland. Hold on!"

The last instruction came in response to a cry from Heide. "*Herr Leutnant*, the formation is altering course! It is heading straight for the coast."

"Jever, latest indications are that the predicted target may be Wilhelmshaven. Alert all squadrons. Repeat, alert all squadrons. Please acknowledge."

There was a pause, and then the lieutenant replaced the handset. "Well, Heide, we've done our bit. It's up to them now. I just hope to God we've got it right, or there will be the devil to pay."

The sentiment was echoed heartily by *Leutnant* Hans Lehmann as, a few minutes later, he tore his *Emil* off the ground at Jever, closely followed by Falcke, his wingman, and four other Messerschmitts of the standby flight. He knew that other pilots of the *Gruppe* who had not been on standby were being rounded up as quickly as possible, but it would be several minutes more before the whole group was airborne. In the meantime, his six aircraft would have to do what they could. As yet, Lehmann had no idea what they were heading into as he led his flight up to 19000 feet, his one thought to get above the enemy formation.

Unlike Lehmann, Armstrong had a very good idea what the Wellington squadron was heading into as it crept closer to Wilhelmshaven, having kept well clear of Heligoland to avoid the heavy anti-aircraft batteries that were known to be there. Around their aircraft, the other Wellingtons in the formation rose and fell gently on the turbulence. Armstrong glanced at Pittaway, who was chewing gum unconcernedly under his oxygen mask, and then looked ahead towards the enemy coast and the approaches to Wilhelmshaven. It was familiar territory.

They were over Wangerooge when the first fighters hit them.

They seemed to come from nowhere, flashing out of the southern sky, arrowing down hard and fast from above to hit the leading formation in a single, devastating pass. Armstrong counted four of them before losing sight of them as they vanished below; a few moments later the excited voice of the rear gunner reported that the Messerschmitts were climbing steeply astern and turning in.

"All right, gunners," Pittaway said over the intercom. "No wild shooting. Let 'em come well within range." He reached across and tapped Armstrong's elbow. "Stand by to take over if I get hit," he added quietly.

Armstrong raised a hand in acknowledgement. With a sick feeling, he was watching the Wellingtons ahead. One of them, the left-hand aircraft, was dropping slowly out of formation, both engines streaming white smoke. It went into a lazy spiral towards the sea. Armstrong did not see any parachutes.

"Fighters coming in astern!" The rear-gunner's yell was followed almost immediately by the clatter of his machine-guns. Armstrong jumped as holes appeared in the bomber's wing between the cockpit and the engine. He crouched in his seat and tried to make himself as inconspicuous as possible, feeling utterly vulnerable and helpless.

It was Lehmann who had attacked Pittaway's Wellington, taking a couple of hits from the rear-gunner in the process. Satisfied that no serious damage had been done, he passed underneath the bomber at speed and then eased back the stick slightly, settling his gunsight squarely on the leading Wellington. Its bulk shuddered in front of him as he opened fire with cannon and machine-guns, raking it from wingtip to wingtip. Immediately, a sheet of white vapour streamed back, eveloping his fighter, its droplets rendering his windscreen opaque. Smelling high-octane fuel, he sheered off to one side hastily and dived away.

Behind him, his wingman, Falcke, also fired a burst into the stricken Wellington. The result was spectacular. The white vapour, pouring from the bomber's holed fuel tanks, erupted into flame.

In the following wave, Armstrong and Pittaway witnessed the whole drama from their cockpit as Wing Commander Goodison's Wellington – for such it was – fell out of formation, wrapped in flame. A few hundred feet lower down, it exploded. They felt the expanding shock-wave like a hammer blow. As Pittaway fought to steady the aircraft, one of the gunners reported that a third Wellington was going down in flames.

Three down out of twelve, Armstrong thought, and we haven't even got as far as Wilhelmshaven. He wondered how Dickie Baird was coping. He was in the bomber on the extreme right of the second flight, and he could see that it was still intact.

Suddenly, there were Messerschmitts everywhere, boaring in from all sides. The noise was unbearable as every gunner opened fire, taking his brief chance to shoot at targets as they streaked past. Acrid fumes drifted through the fuselage. The bomb aimer, crouched in his nose position, reported that Wilhelmshaven was dead ahead, but that he could not see any ships in the anchorage.

"That's torn it," said Pittaway, talking to himself. At the briefing, they had been told that if they couldn't find any warships to bomb, they were to bring their bombs back.

The Wellington bucked and jolted as the formation flew on through yellow-grey smoke of heavy anti-aircraft bursts. By some sort of miracle, none of the bombers was hit.

The formation flew on over Wilhelmshaven and then turned out towards the open sea again, still carrying its bombs. All of a sudden the flak died away. Then the fighters came in again.

Chapter Eight

"I see they've let you out, then."

Armstrong looked up from his armchair in the Mess ante-room to see Pittaway looking down at him. The New Zealander gave a weary smile. "You look bloody awful," he said.

Armstrong placed an experimental hand on the bandage that swathed his head and winced, eyeing Pittaway's left arm, which was in a sling.

"Thanks. You don't look all that hot yourself. I still can't remember a damned thing after we jettisoned our bombs."

"You flew us back," Pittaway told him. "I wasn't much use with a couple of bullets through this." He pointed to his injured arm. "You also crashed," he added reproachfully.

"Crash-landed," Armstrong corrected him, "or so I'm told. Still, every landing you walk away from is a good one."

"You didn't walk away," Pittaway objected. "You were bloody well carried. Out cold, you were. Anyway, what's the damage?"

"Oh, just a cut on the dome and a bit of concussion," Armstrong said. "I was lucky. We all were."

"You can say that again," said Pittaway, with considerable feeling. "What a God-almighty cock-up!"

Armstrong made no reply. He knew the story, even the bits his mind had blanked out, from conversations he had overheard, even though no one had been willing to come straight out and tell him. Three Wellingtons had come back out of the twelve; his had been the only one to make it back to base, the other two having landed at other airfields. Dickie Baird had been in one of the missing aircraft.

Pittaway looked at the clock on the ante-room wall. It was five past twelve. Outside, a thick fog lay over the aerodrome.

"Fancy a couple of beers and a spot of lunch?" he asked. Armstrong shook his head.

"No. Not here, anyway." Pittaway nodded. He knew what the other was thinking. Things were depressing enough, without having to sit and stare at the empty spaces in the dining-room. It would be the same in the other messes too, he reflected, for the bulk of the Wellingtons' crews had been made up of sergeants and aircraftmen.

"You reckon you can drive my jalopy?" The New Zealander's question took Armstrong by surprise. "I suppose so," he said dubiously, eyeing the fog outside. "Exactly what did you have in mind?"

"A bit of rape and pillage," said Pittaway, "or alternatively, if your bonce isn't up to that, a sandwich or two in Cambridge and some falling-down drunk. Nobody's going to need us for anything, are they?"

Armstrong had to agree with him. "The doc said no alcohol, though."

Pittaway snorted. "That's what he said to me, too. Bugger it. Are we going to give it a try?"

"Why not? Booze is as good a pain-killer as any." He levered himself painfully out of his chair, conscious that the bruises that covered a large area of his body hurt far more than his head did. The two officers collected their greatcoats, told the Mess receptionist of their intentions, and went out into the cold, damp fog, where Armstrong was introduced to Pittaway's means of transport, a Morgan three-wheeler.

Armstrong wanted to take a look at the remains of their Wellington, so they called briefly at the Watch Office to obtain permission to drive across the airfield. Since nothing was flying, nor likely to be in the immediate future, there were no objections.

The Wellington lay close to the airfield perimeter, a grey, broken ghost surrounded by wraiths of swirling fog. They walked around it slowly, Armstrong seeing the damage it had suffered for the first time. The aircraft lay on its belly at the end of a swathe of churned-up earth. Pittaway told his companion, who could not remember, that despite frantic efforts the undercarriage had refused to come down. There were rents in the wings where bullets had torn their way through, and strips of fabric dangled from the fuselage, revealing the criss-cross girders of the main frame. Armstrong marvelled that anyone had got out alive.

"Come on," he said. "I really need that drink now."

It took them the best part of an hour to crawl through the murk to the Blue Bells, which was deserted. Phyllis was behind the bar. She looked at the newcomers with consternation.

"Gawd!" she exclaimed. "What happened to you two?"

"We fell off our bicycles," Pittaway said laconically. "You must be the lovely Phyllis. This bloke's been doing nothing but sing your praises." He motioned in the direction of his embarrassed companion with his free thumb. The barmaid simpered and fluttered her eyelashes at Armstrong, who turned bright red and became suddenly tongue-tied.

The New Zealander looked around at the empty room and asked where everyone was. "Potato-picking," Phyllis told him. "Busy time of the year, this is."

"Rather them than me," Pittaway said. The barmaid placed their beers in front of them and looked at him with mild curiosity. "Are you an Australian?" she wanted to know. The pilot drew himself up to his full five feet seven inches and glared at her in mock anger. "Madam, how dare you! I am a New Zealander, I will have you know, the citizen of a land filled with wonder and beauty."

"And sheep," Armstrong murmured, his face in his beer mug.

"Leave my sex life out of it," Pittaway said. Phyllis looked aghast. "Now then, gents, that's no way to talk. We'll have no smut in here, thanks very much."

She adopted a prim expression and turned her back on them to polish some glasses. In the bar mirror they caught sight of her expression. She was grinning.

They chatted for half an hour about nothing in particular, exchanging pleasantries with one or two farming folk who wandered in, then Pittaway had a sudden thought. "I reckon we'll be in for a spot of leave," he said. "Where's home?"

"Berwick-on-Tweed," Armstrong informed him.

Pittaway nodded. "Oh, yeah, right up on the Scottish border. Flown over it a few times when I was doing my training. Isn't that where the Scots and English used to fight one another all the time?"

"Something like that," Armstrong said. "They were a pretty nasty lot by all accounts, too. There's a story, for instance, about one of the English kings besieging Berwick – Edward the First, I think it was – who put it about that any Scot who let in the English army would be given his weight in gold. Some chap fell for it, and when he'd opened the gate and let the English in they poured molten gold down his neck."

"Nice people," Pittaway said with a raised eyebrow. "You haven't got a Scots accent, though. How's that? I've come across people of Scottish extraction who've lived in New Zealand for generations and they've still got an accent you could cut with a knife."

"If I've got an accent at all, it's Northumbrian," Armstrong said. "It all depends where you were brought up. The river Tweed runs right through the middle of Berwick, so on the north side you're a Scot, on the south a Northumbrian. My family were border rievers," he added, smiling.

"Border what?"

"Rievers. They used to go around doing people in, stealing their livestock and so on. Everybody was at it in the olden days up on the borders. They ran protection rackets that made Al Capone look like an amateur. The word 'blackmail' originated on the borders; it means 'black rent', in other words the extortion money people used to have to pay to my ancestors and their chums if they wanted to keep their heads on their shoulders."

"I don't think I want to know you," Pittaway said, eyeing his companion in mock horror. "Better have another couple of beers, quick, Phyllis."

The barmaid was about to serve them when a telephone jangled somewhere. She excused herself and went through a door that led from the bar to a small, private parlour. A couple of minutes later she returned and told Armstrong that there was a telephone call for him. She had no idea who was on the other end of the line.

"It's probably your murky past catching up with you," Pittaway said as Phyllis ushered Armstrong through the counter flap that gave access to the area behind the bar, and the room beyond.

"No such luck," Armstrong answered. "More likely it's the doc, who's found out where we are and is about to raise hell."

But the voice on the telephone didn't belong to the Station Medical Officer. It belonged to Dickie Baird.

The naval officer came in 40 minutes later and ordered a large gin. He swallowed it in a single gulp and ordered another. Only then did he address Armstrong and Pittaway.

"They told me I'd find you here," he said, eyeing their respective injuries. "A rough ride, was it?"

"Bloody hell, Dickie!" Armstrong burst out. "Never mind about us. What about you? We thought you were a goner! Come on, what's the story?"

"Not much to it, really," Baird told them modestly. "Our fuel tanks were holed to hell, but they didn't catch fire, thank God. They just kept on losing fuel until it ran out, somewhere off the Zuider Zee. Luckily, the fighters had long since given up on us; they must have been short of fuel too, I guess."

Baird eyed his gin, took a sip, then continued: "Anyway, the skipper pulled off an absolutely first-class ditching and we all got out OK except for the rear gunner, who had a smashed kneecap. The poor devil was in a lot of pain, but we got him into the dinghy and sat there, pretty wet and miserable and expecting to be picked up by the Huns. As it turned out, a Dutch trawler came along after a while and hauled us in. The crew filled us full of brandy, gave us something to eat, and a few hours later they rendezvoused with one of our boats and handed us over. We landed at Lowestoft. And that was that."

"Talk about luck!" Pittaway said. "They should have interned you, by rights. After all, the Dutch are neutral."

"So they are," Baird agreed. "They also dislike the Huns, as we discovered. Well, here's to the Dutch fishing fleet." He despatched his gin and turned to Phyllis to order his third.

"Hang on a minute, dear," the barmaid said. "Something's up."

Her voice was full of concern, and they saw that she was looking at a man who had just entered the room. He was elderly, and Armstrong vaguely remembered that he had been one of the domino players when he had visited the inn previously. The man's usually weathered face was white, and he tottered to the bar as though intoxicated.

"For God's sake, Phyllis, give me a whisky." His voice was hoarse and tremulous.

"George, whatever's the matter?" The barmaid asked. "You look quite done in." He looked at her with eyes that were filled with tears.

"They've sunk the *Courageous*, he whispered. "The buggers have sunk the *Courageous*. I've had a telegram. . . ." His voice tailed away miserably.

"Oh, God!" Phyllis's hand flew to her mouth and her eyes widened in horror. "John's ship?"

The old man nodded dumbly, choking back sobs. "Aye. My lad's ship. I got a telegram. . . ."

"Excuse me, Sir." Baird gently took the old man's elbow. "Did you say the *Courageous* – the aircraft carrier? She's my ship, too."

The old man looked at him for the first time. Baird saw that tears were coursing down his cheeks. "Not any more she's not, son. They've sunk her. Torpedoed, she was. Heavy loss of life, they said.

My lad's gone. He was all I had. Did you know him, then, son? John Farmer. Able Seaman." There was a plea in his voice, a longing to establish a contact, however slender, with a past that was lost forever.

Baird nodded. "Yes, I knew him," he lied. "A very fine sailor, and a great asset to the ship."

"Aye. Aye, I thought you would. Everybody knew John." He picked up the glass of whisky that Phyllis had set in front of him and drank deeply. He wiped his mouth with the back of his hand, then said: "Listen, son, would you mind coming home with me for a few minutes? Maybe you'd like to see some photographs . . . I'd like to talk to somebody, just for a little while. My missus is dead, you see. . . ."

"Of course. I'd be glad to. Shall we go now?"

They left the room together, Baird making a silent gesture to his companions that said: What else can I do? The others nodded, understanding. Phyllis turned away, crying silently.

Later, they learned that the carrier had been sunk by a U-boat in the Western Approaches, and that over 500 of her crew had gone down with her. And so the cold hand of war touched this quiet, cosy backwater for the first time, leaving its fingerprints on the ravaged face of an old man who would never see his son again.

Chapter Nine

Life was full of little surprises, Armstrong reflected, and a place called Wick in the grip of a January snowstorm must surely be one of the nastiest. Sticking out like a pimple on the north-east tip of Scotland, the place was subject to every kind of unpleasant weather the Arctic winds chose to hurl at it.

He had reported back to Deanland in December following his stint with Bomber Command, and after a fortnight spent kicking his heels around the airfield with nothing to do – the promised Spitfires having still not materialised – he had been sent off on leave by Wing Commander Royston. So, astride his trusty Norton – which to his relief he had found none the worse for its weeks of enforced idleness – he had ridden north to Berwick to spend Christmas with his parents.

He had not really enjoyed his leave. His father, anxious to show him off at his local pub, couldn't understand why Armstrong disliked being bought round after round of drinks while never being allowed to put his hand in his own pocket; nor could he understand why the pilot tended to become irritable when his mother and sister fussed over him. How could Armstrong explain that he was embarrassed not by the attention, but by the fact that his mother was obviously putting on a brave face, and by the knowledge that she was secretly willing every minute of his leave to extend into hours, and every hour into days? How could he explain the difficulty in making small talk with his sister's boyfriend, a Royal Artillery gunner serving with a nearby coastal battery?

There was nothing of the snob in Armstrong. It had taken his father to put his feelings into words.

"The war's changing you, son. It's to be expected. We all go through it. You can spend years in the forces and never alter a bit, but action makes a man different. I don't know what you are up to, but you didn't get that medal for nothing. Try to relax a bit, and be patient with your mother. She worries about you. And there's Jean. She's hardly had a word from you since war broke out."

In that, he was right; Armstrong had only written two or three times to his girlfriend since last August, when he had first arrived at Deanland. He felt bad about that now, for Jean deserved better. She was a librarian, a gentle, quiet girl who had been his friend since schooldays. He felt a deep affection for her, but he had never made the mistake of confusing it with love – although he felt sure that she loved him, in her own way. He was sexually attracted to her, but his occasional foray up the sexual path with her had always ended at a brick wall; it bore a big sign that said "This far, but no further." The end result, for him, had been frustration, and for her an apologetic shyness.

The trouble was that his feelings for her were now tainted by guilt, for Phyllis had shown him what the real thing could be like. The first time it had happened they had both had too much to drink, but on subsequent occasions it had happened because they had both wanted it to. No, he thought, his leave had not been a truly happy time; and Phyllis was still in Cambridge, while he was stuck in this God-forsaken Scottish outpost.

The telegram ordering him to Wick had arrived on the second day of January, its content cutting through an exceedingly bad hangover. Wisely, he had decided to leave his motor cycle at his parents' house, and had taken the train north. The train had been dirty and overcrowded, filled mostly with comatose sailors returning from leave and a few civilians who grumbled constantly because they were unable to get seats. Change at Edinburgh; change again at Dundee, and again at Aberdeen, and yet again at Inverness; what a bloody nightmare of a journey!

And Wick airfield itself: that was pretty nightmarish, too, a slushy quagmire with half-completed tarmac runways, only one of which was operational, and three canvas hangars. It looked like a construction site, which it was. The Officers' and NCOs' Messes were wooden huts, the accommodation areas radiating from a central bar and dining area, like spokes around the hub of a wheel.

The airfield, thought Armstrong, was not exactly

over-populated, even though it had recently assumed the role of a Fighter Command Sector Station. Sector HQ was in a nearby elementary school. Every now and then, Armstrong understood, a flight of Spitfires or Hurricanes turned up to form an air defence detachment, stayed for a few days, then went away again. There were none there at the moment. The "resident" air defence force seemed to be four Blackburn Skua fighters of the Fleet Air Arm's No 803 Squadron, and a few Avro Ansons of No 269 Squadron carried out patrols around the coastline to Cape Wrath and occasionally went as far as the Faeroes when the weather was flyable, which it had not been for some days.

Armstrong had been allocated a small office in Station Headquarters. He sat in it now, gazing moodily at the swirling snowflakes through a gap he had rubbed in the frosted window pane and feeling like a lost soul, time and boredom settling on his shoulders like a ton weight. He knew what he had to do, but the weather thwarted him. He wished with all his heart that it would break. The bleakness of Caithness was utterly depressing.

Damn it, anything was better than this! Making up his mind suddenly, he set down his half-finished mug of coffee – it was cold anyway – on the desk and put on his greatcoat. Taking his cap from a hook, he went out into the corridor, locking the office door behind him. Pausing only to stick his head into the Orderly Room to tell the duty corporal where he was going – not that anyone was likely to want him – he put on his cap, turned up his coat collar and left the building by a side entrance.

Large, damp snowflakes settled on him as he walked quickly along the track – for it was no more than that – leading to the hangars. As he drew near them, he was challenged by a snowman with a rifle and bayonet: a luckless sentry doing his stint on watch. Satisfied that Armstrong wasn't a company of German paratroopers, the man let him pass.

The hangar was well lit. Armstrong shook the snow off himself and nodded to some naval air mechanics who were working on a Skua's engine. Then his eyes lit upon the object of his visit.

She stood alone at the far end of the hangar in all her beauty, segregated from the main area by a rope attached to an array of oil drums and a large sign that proclaimed: KEEP CLEAR – NO UNAUTHORISED PERSONS PAST THIS POINT. Her upper surfaces were painted pale blue; her undersides were white. She carried no armament; only two F.24 cameras, mounted in her fuselage and pointing vertically downwards. She had been delivered just before the onset of the bad weather by a member of the Air Transport Auxiliary – who had turned out, much to everyone's surprise, to be an extremely attractive blonde called Diana. She had dined that evening in the Mess, politely tolerated the attentions of the young Fleet Air Arm pilots who had clustered around her like wasps around a pot of jam, gone to bed, and departed by train the next morning. Armstrong had exchanged a few words with her, and that was all.

Since then, because of the weather, there had been the opportunity for no more than a few circuits around the aerodrome – enough for Armstrong once again to revel in the feel of a Spitfire under his touch. But this was no ordinary Spitfire. Stripped of the usual eight machine-guns and radio and therefore lighter than the standard Mk I of her breed, she would fly at 35,000 feet with ease. She had a Rolls-Royce Merlin III engine, the best available. The gun ports in the leading edges of the wings were filled by metal plates and every crack in her external surfaces was blocked by plaster of paris. She was polished all over to a hard, sleek gloss, and an extra fuel tank fitted behind the cockpit gave her a range of 800 miles or more. In practical terms, that meant that she could cover the whole area from northern Scotland to the Norwegian Sea and across to Iceland, the happy hunting ground for the German surface raiders and submarines. She was called the Spitfire PR1B, she was the first of her kind, and she was Armstrong's.

Armstrong stepped over the protective ropes and walked around the Spitfire, checking that all was well. He did it every day, even though he was aware that his ground crew did exactly the same thing each morning, running his hands over the smoothness of her wings and fuselage, taking in her heady perfume of paint and oil and petrol and aluminium, the typical smell of a thoroughbred aircraft.

Her wings were cold to the touch, and a sudden chill passed through him, transmitted not by the metal, but by the foreknowledge of the tasks he would soon have to perform. Flights lasting for hours on end, cramped in the Spitfire's tiny cockpit, with a single engine, all that stood between him and the merciless winter sea. . . .

. . . the sea. Three miles below him it stretched away to a curved horizon, a sheet of blue-grey glass shot here and there with whorls and eddies of green. Far away, to the north, where the sea and sky mingled, there was a reflection of white and pink, where the sun's rays touched the ice floes that drifted over the barren seas between Norway's North Cape and Jan Mayen Island.

It was fearsomely cold in the cockpit, despite the array of clothing Armstrong was wearing. He couldn't help smiling to himself as he mentally checked off his clothing inventory. On his feet he wore a pair of ladies' silk stockings (Phyllis would no doubt have laughed if she had known the use he was making of her little parting keepsake), a pair of football stockings, a pair of oiled Scandinavian ski socks and RAF-issue fur-lined boots. On his hands were two pairs of RAF silk gloves and some special fur-backed and fur-lined gauntlets which he had purchased himself; he had cut off the fingertips, for it was essential to retain some fingertip control, particularly for the camera control box. He wore his normal RAF uniform with a thick vest, roll-neck sweater and a thing called a Tropal lining which was stuffed with a kind of kapok. All this, he thought, was what the well-dressed photo-recce pilot was compelled to wear in early February, 1940.

The black crags of the Norwegian coast were far away to starboard. He was approaching the limit of the Spitfire's combat radius, and so far he had seen precious little to justify this sortie; just a few fishing boats and some friendly destroyers, which had opened fire on him in a most unfriendly fashion.

He pondered on what to do. To the north-west lay Iceland and the Denmark Strait, the route taken to and from the Atlantic by enemy ships; there was nothing visible in that direction, and so he turned east, towards Norway. He checked his position by dead reckoning, and realized with a sudden shock that he must be poised almost directly over the Arctic Circle. A momentary twinge of fear went through him with the knowledge that he had flown farther north than he had ever been before, an irrational dread that the freezing sea and sky would swallow him up. It passed in moments, and he never experienced such a feeling again.

He altered course again, south-eastwards this time, scanning the surface of the sea ahead and below. His brief was to photograph any vessel that might be identified as a tanker. Why, he had no idea.

He held his course for 40 minutes, converging slowly on the Norwegian coastline. He was close enough now to pick out definite landmarks, and a glance at his map told him that the islands he could see ahead were those sheltering the approaches to Trondheimsfjord.

In the open sea north-west of the islands, something moved. It was a large ship, trailing a herring-bone wake. Keeping his eyes on the vessel all the time – it was still no more than a dot – Armstrong began to lose height, switching on the camera equipment as he did so and turning the time interval between exposures down to the bare minimum. If the vessel was a tanker – and it was certainly beginning to look like one – he wanted to get as many frames as possible in a single run overhead.

His mind registered the details of the ship as he sped towards it from astern. It was a tanker all right, with its long foredeck and a single funnel aft.

He roared over it at a height of only a few hundred feet, cameras in action, and caught a glimpse of some seamen on the deck, looking up at him. The ship was well inside Norwegian territorial waters and appeared to be heading directly for Trondheim.

He pulled up, gained height in a climbing turn and decided to make a second run from the beam. He passed over the ship in a flash, but there was time to make out the name in large white letters on her stern: *Altmark*.

So that was what it was all about, Armstrong thought as he climbed away over the sea, conscious that he had just about enough fuel left to get back to his base. *Altmark*: the supply tanker for the German battleship *Admiral Graf Spee*, hounded by British warships to take refuge in Montevideo harbour and then scuttled by her captain, Langsdorff, last December.

Well, he had found the tanker, and he felt a

deep inner satisfaction; but he had no idea why the Admiralty should have set such store in locating her. As far as he was aware – according to rumour at least – half of Coastal Command and the the Home Fleet had been out in search of the elusive vessel ever since word had come in that she had left her South Atlantic station and was heading home to Germany. Why all the effort, when there were major German warships to be tracked down and destroyed?

It was a couple of weeks more before he knew. He was seated at the breakfast table one morning when one of the Coastal Command Anson pilots, a flight lieutenant called Terry Layton, plonked himself down on the chair opposite, a broad grin on his face. He brandished a copy of one of the morning newspapers.

"Seen this?" he asked. Armstrong shook his head, chewing on a mouthful of egg. Layton folded the paper in half and pushed it across the table, turning it so that Armstrong could read it. Frowning, Armstrong peered over his plate at the news item Layton was indicating with his finger. The piece was dated a couple of days earlier.

> THE ROYAL NAVY'S NELSON TOUCH! the headline proclaimed. DARING RESCUE BY BRITISH WARSHIPS.
>
> The Admiralty announced today that 300 Merchant Navy sailors, taken prisoner by the German pocket battleship *Admiral Graf Spee*, have been rescued from captivity aboard the

infamous prison ship *Altmark* in a bold operation by destroyers of the Royal Navy.

The *Altmark*, homeward bound for Germany, had taken refuge in a Norwegian fjord in contravention of all the rules of Norwegian neutrality. She was pursued there by destroyers of the Home Fleet, whose crews released all the captives after a short fight in which several Germans are reported to have been killed and wounded. There were no British casualties, and all our warships withdrew safely from Norwegian waters. We hope to publish a more detailed report in tomorrow's edition.

Armstrong leaned back in his chair and scratched his head. "Well, I'll be damned!" he exclaimed. "So that's what it was all about. I can't help feeling rather pleased," he added, smiling at the man opposite.

"I'll bet old Adolf isn't," Layton said. "It's a fair old smack in the eye for him. The last straw, I shouldn't wonder."

It was a prophetic remark, although neither of them realized it at the time.

Chapter Ten

FUHRER HEADQUARTERS,
1 MARCH 1940
MOST SECRET
DIRECTIVE FOR OPERATION
"WESER EXERCISE"

The development of the situation in Scandinavia requires the making of all preparations for the occupation of Denmark and Norway. This operation should prevent British encroachment on Scandinavia and the Baltic. Further it should guarantee our ore base in Sweden and give our Navy and the Air Force a wider starting line against Britain. In view of our military and political power in comparison with that of the Scandinavian States, the force to be employed in WESER EXERCISE will be kept as small as possible. The numerical weakness will be balanced by daring actions and surprise execution.

On principle, we will do our utmost to make the operation appear as a peaceful occupation, the object of which is the military protection of the neutrality of the Scandinavian States.

Corresponding demands will be transmitted to the Governments at the beginning of the occupation. If necessary, demonstrations by the Navy and Air Force will provide the necessary emphasis. If, in spite of this, resistance should be met, all military means will be used to crush it. The crossing of the Danish border and the landings in Norway must take place simultaneously.

It is most important that the Scandinavian States as well as the Western opponents should be taken by surprise. The troops may be acquainted with the actual objectives only after putting to sea.

Adolf Hitler.

"He's good at taking people by surprise," General Nikolaus von Falkenhorst remarked mildly as he glanced at the directive. "He certainly took *me* by surprise."

It was less than two weeks since Falkenhorst, quite out of the blue, had been appointed to mastermind the forthcoming invasion of Scandinavia. Before that, he had been leading a fairly quiet life as commander of an Army Group on the Western Front. The appointment had come, he knew, because of his successful conduct of operations in Finland back in 1918, at the very end of the Great War.

Falkenhorst's aide, a grey-haired colonel who had served under him in that half-forgotten campaign, smiled as he poured his superior a cup of coffee. The general's first act after his appointment, he recalled, had been to go out and buy a Baedeker travel guide so that he could find out what Norway was like. From this, he had worked out a plan whereby one division would occupy each of Norway's five main harbours, Oslo, Stavanger, Bergen, Trondheim and Narvik. The plan was sketchy at best, but it had been enough to satisfy Hitler. Falkenhorst had been sworn to secrecy, then simply told to get on with it.

He and his staff had put in a great deal of work in the past couple of weeks, assembling the forces necessary for the invasion. The task had not been without its arguments; the Army High Command was not happy about having several divisions stripped from other areas, and the fat Field Marshal Goering, the Luftwaffe C-in-C, was known to be furious because he had not been consulted beforehand.

Despite all the problems, the WESER EXERCISE plan was pretty well complete. All it needed now was a date – and above all, a motive. What worried Falkenhorst most of all was that if the Germans didn't make a surprise move quickly against Norway, the British might beat them to it. He wondered how much they already knew, or suspected, of Germany's intentions.

"The fact is," Wing Commander Royston said, "that we have no clear idea of what the Huns are up to. We can bring back all the photographs that are asked of us; what they don't tell our Intelligence people is when or where the Germans might attack. I'm sure of one thing, though," he added grimly, "when they do attack, be it on the Western Front or Scandinavia, they will do it hard and fast. There'll be little or no warning."

Royston had spent the last few weeks at an airfield in France, together with another photo-reconnaissance pilot. The PR flight now had three Spitfires and four pilots and was once again concentrated on Deanland, although Armstrong had a feeling that it would not be for long.

"There's a rumour going around in France that the Huns had actually planned an offensive in the west for last January," Royston continued, "but that it came unstuck when one of their communications aircraft strayed across the Belgian frontier and made a forced landing. There was a staff officer in it, and he was carrying the German war plan, or so the story goes. I don't know how true it is."

In fact, it was completely true. On the morning of 10 January 1940, Major Hellmuth Reinberger, a German paratroop officer, had been *en route* from Loddenheide to Cologne in a Messerschmitt 108 when the pilot, Erich Hoenmanns, encountered deteriorating weather. Before long, with the visibility decreasing all the time, Hoenmanns realized that he was hopelessly lost and that without knowing it he had probably been driven across the Rhine, miles off track, by a strong easterly wind.

The pilot at once changed course, heading east in the hope of sighting the river. A minute later the engine began to misfire; the carburettor was icing up. Hoenmanns juggled with the engine controls, but it was no use. Soon the engine cut out altogether, and he was left with no alternative but to make a forced landing.

Selecting a large, snow-covered field, he turned into wind and began his approach. At the last moment the pilot spotted a line of poplars in his path. It was too late to avoid them; all he could do was kick the rudder frantically and steer for what looked like a sizeable gap. A second later the aircraft shook violently as the trees whipped off both its wingtips; then it was down, lurching over the snow and coming to rest just short of the far hedge.

The two men scrambled from the cockpit with no worse injury than a severe shaking. After consulting their map, they decided that they had landed near Mechelen, in Belgian territory. Reinberger immediately took shelter behind the hedge and set about trying to burn the contents of his briefcase – no less a document than CASE YELLOW, the operational order for the invasion of France and the Low Countries. His lighter failed to work, and he had almost given up in despair when a Belgian peasant came up and obligingly offered him a match, with the aid of which he soon had a small fire going.

He was feeding the papers into it, sheet by sheet, when he heard shouts. Coming towards the crippled aircraft across the field were some Belgian soldiers. Hoenmanns, hoping to buy enough time to enable Reinberger to finish his task, went to meet them half-way with his hands up in an attempt to convince them that he had been alone in the aircraft. However, a keen-eyed Belgian soon spotted the ribbon of smoke rising from behind the hedge, and a minute later Reinberger had been captured too – together with the documents, most of which were still intact.

The two men were taken to a nearby police post, where they were interrogated by a Belgian intelligence officer. During the proceedings, Reinberger saw that the documents were lying on a table nearby. He seized them and tried to thrust them into a stove, but they were rescued – scorched but still legible – by the Belgian officer.

Copies of the documents were quickly passed on to the Dutch and French governments. The latter at once placed its armies in a state of alert, and the French First Army Group, moving through fearful conditions of snow and ice, closed up to the Belgian frontier, having been advised by the Belgian High Command that the necessary authority would be given for Allied forces to enter Belgian territory. This order, however, was immediately countermanded by Belgium's King Leopold, and the French had no alternative but to pull back once more.

Meanwhile, Hitler had been informed of the incident on the morning of 11 January. He at once flew into one of his characteristic rages, threatening the death sentence for both Hoenmanns and Reinberger. Within 48 hours reports were reaching the German High Command of Belgian and Dutch mobilization, together with large-scale movements by the French Army. That same day, with the weather once again deteriorating, Hitler gave orders for the indefinite postponement of CASE YELLOW.

It is by such chance happenings, on the turn of

a card or the throw of the dice, that the course of history is dictated. The attack in the West would wait until the summer; Hitler's first objectives now would be Denmark and Norway.

Royston and Armstrong were sitting in the former's office, chatting about the war situation in general. On the Continent of Europe the opposing armies still eyed one another from behind their respective fortifications and did nothing, but in the air it was a different story. There, the war was for real, and the reconnaissance aircraft of both sides were having a particularly hard time, as Royston explained.

"It's the French who are suffering the most," he told Armstrong. "Their main recce type is a twin-engined bird called a Potez 63; it's badly underarmed and the 109s have been knocking them down like flies. There's a squadron of them at Seclin, where we were, and crew morale is at rock bottom. They're taking the same kind of knocks that our recce Blenheims took earlier on, only worse. They would give anything to have something like the Spitfire."

"What are the French fighters like?" Armstrong wanted to know. His companion grimaced.

"Pretty poor. Their main type is the Morane 406, and it's no match for the Me 109. Just before we left Seclin, 11 Moranes from a squadron based up the road were bounced by 109s over the frontier and five of them were shot down. The best French fighter is actually American – the Curtiss Hawk, a nippy litle radial-engined machine. They don't have many of them, though."

He gazed thoughtfully out of the window. It was the first week of April, and the weather was dreadful. The rain was lashing down under a leaden sky and the windsock on the airfield boundary stuck out stiffly from its pole as strong gusts of wind battered at it.

"Our Hurricanes are the best fighter asset over there," Royston continued, "but there are only four squadrons of them – two with the Air Component and two with the AASF." The Air Component's task was to defend the British Expeditionary Force in France, while the AASF, the Advanced Air Striking Force, was equipped mainly with Fairey Battle light bombers. The two AASF Hurricane squadrons, Nos 1 and 73, were to provide top cover for the Battles if and when the latter were required to go into action.

"That New Zealand chap's with one of the AASF Hurricane squadrons, isn't he? You know, the one who's been in the news lately."

Royston nodded in response to Armstrong's comment. "That's right. Cobber Kain. He's building up quite a reputation for himself. He's got 11 or 12 Huns to his credit so far. As a matter of fact, I've met him. I dropped into 73 Squadron's base at Rouvres a couple of weeks ago. He'd just had a pretty narrow squeak. He didn't mention it himself, but his squadron commander told me about it."

"What happened?"

"Well, Kain and a sergeant pilot were patrolling the front line at 20,000 feet – they'd been escorting a Potez on a recce mission – when they sighted some anti-aircraft bursts over Thionville and flew towards them. A minute later Kain spotted seven Heinkels about 5000 feet higher up and went after them, leaving his number two behind in the process. As he gained on the Heinkels, he heard his number two shout a warning that half a dozen Me 109s were coming down on them. Kain looked around just in time to see a 109 blazing away at him; he broke away, but not before he'd taken some cannon shells through his rear fuselage. Then he was attacked by a second 109, which also hit him, but it overshot and he clobbered it as it went past.

"By this time Kain was miles inside Germany, so he started a turn towards our lines – at which point he was attacked by a third Messerschmitt. His engine stopped with a loud bang and smoke filled the cockpit. He couldn't see his compass, so he pointed his aircraft in what he hoped was the direction of Metz and trimmed her for a long glide, turning his oxygen full on so that he could breathe. By the time he crossed the front line flames were starting to break through into the cockpit, but he managed to make an emergency landing on a French airfield."

"Somebody was obviously on his side," Armstrong said. He knew that it must have needed exceptional nerve to stay with an aircraft that was on fire. He gave an involuntary shudder; one of his private nightmares involved being trapped in a Spitfire that was burning, particularly a photo-recce Spitfire, with its extra fuel tanks. He had worked out that he would have about seven seconds in which to unfasten his seat harness, unplug his R/T and oxygen leads, slide back the canopy and get out before the cockpit became a raging inferno.

A knock at the door interrupted his somewhat depressing reverie. A moment later Max, the Lithuanian, entered the office, silently handed a piece of paper to Royston, then departed without saying a word, nodding and smiling at Armstrong in friendly fashion as he passed by.

It was a message slip. Royston studied it, his face serious, then folded it and put it in his pocket. He took time to light a cigarette before speaking.

"Intelligence reports that heavy units of the German Fleet are putting to sea," he told Armstrong. "To my mind, that can only mean one of two possibilities. Either they are planning a major breakout into the North Atlantic, or we've got an invasion of Norway on our hands. We are to move up to Kinloss as soon as the weather lifts."

Armstrong's heart sank. North of the border again, he groaned inwardly. Still, at least it's not bloody Wick. He looked out at the lowering clouds and the rain; for the time being, nothing was going anywhere.

Chapter Eleven

Southern Norway, 9 April 1940: 04.45 hours

On this Tuesday morning, the second Tuesday in April, the waters of Oslofjord and its adjacent hillsides were shrouded in fog. It was not yet five o'clock, but already people were up and about, for there were breakfasts to be prepared, nets to be made ready, and engines to be checked before the fishing boats could put to sea on the morning tide. An eerie silence hung over everything, as it always did when fog clung to the water. Somewhere, a muffled bell tolled, and a siren gave a couple of mournful blasts, as though in answer.

Even the great, booming explosions that came reverberating without warning over the fjord were deadened by the grey vapour. The fishermen on the quaysides paused at their work and looked at one another in alarm, knowing the sound for what it was. The great guns of the Feste Oskarsborg, the fortress that guarded the Drobak Narrows and the approaches to Oslo, fired practice rounds from time to time, but never at this hour of the morning. The explosions thundered out again and again, splitting the silence in a continuous drumfire that showed no sign of ending. What, the fishing folk asked themselves and one another, was going on out there, in the darkness and the murk?

Daylight came, and with it a slight lifting of the fog, enough to reveal a fantastic sight. Oslofjord was crammed with ships of all kinds – warships, freighters, troopships. At the entrance to Drobak Narrows a tall column of smoke rose into the sky, penetrating the fog like a dark finger. At its base, surrounded by spreading oil, licked by flames and on her beam ends, lay the German heavy cruiser *Blücher*, hit by several torpedoes from the Oskarsborg defences, on fire and sinking. Nearby, other cruisers and destroyers duelled with the fortress, trying to blast a path through the narrows so that the troopships – penned up at the moment in a dangerous bottleneck – could break through into Oslo harbour.

As the sun rose, and the fog drifted into ridge-like banks that made tracts of southern Norway visible from the air, waves of three-engined Junkers 52 transports came droning in across the Skagerrak. Ahead of them, Messerschmitt 110 fighters swept the sky, ready to eliminate any resistance. Their task was hardly formidable. The Royal Norwegian Army Air Force had only nine fighters, Gloster Gladiator biplanes, and on this ninth day of April only seven of them were airworthy. The Messerschmitts raced across Fornebu, Oslo's airport, and caught two of the Gladiators on the ground, destroying them with cannon fire, then circled the airfield watchfully, diving down from time to time to strafe Norwegian machine-gun posts, while the first of the Junkers 52 transports touched down to disgorge their airborne troops.

High over Oslo the five surviving Gladiators, which had managed to take off before the onslaught began, fought on. In a savage engagement with a mass of enemy bombers they destroyed two Heinkel 111s and a Dornier 17, but one Gladiator was shot down – its pilot miraculously surviving – and two more had to be abandoned when, short of fuel, they landed on a frozen lake to the north of the capital. The remaining two, their ammunition exhausted, withdrew to an airstrip farther north.

While the airborne troops consolidated their position at Fornebu and prepared to advance on Oslo, another formation of Junkers transports battled its way through bad weather to Stavanger, in south-west Norway. Jumping from only 400 feet, 150 heavily-armed paratroops descended on Stavanger airfield, which was in their hands within half an hour.

Earlier, another German airborne force had landed at Aalborg, in Denmark. That country, overwhelmed by surprise, was now being occupied fairly peacefully; its airfields and ports would be vital for the continued supply of the Norwegian invasion forces.

There had been plenty of warning of the Germans' intentions. For several days in early April, the British Government had been receiving intelligence reports of unusual enemy activity in the Baltic ports, and had interpreted this as a sign that heavy units of the German Fleet were preparing to break out into the Atlantic. As it happened, the interpretation was completely wrong. The bulk of the enemy invasion force was already at sea on 7 April, ploughing northwards through savage weather. In the troopships, soldiers who had never seen the sea before, men who had no idea where they were going until they embarked – some thought Scotland, and made jokes about the whisky in an attempt to lift morale amid the stench and misery of seasickness – were battered helplessly against the iron bulkheads.

This part of the invasion force was divided into three Task Groups. Group One, with Narvik as its objective, had the farthest distance to travel – roughly 1000 miles – and was heavily escorted by the battlecruisers *Scharnhorst* and *Gneisenau*, together with ten destroyers; Group Two, bound for Trondheim, was guarded by the cruiser *Admiral Hipper* and four destroyers, while Group Three, heading for Bergen, was protected by the cruisers *Köln* and *Königsberg*, screened by torpedo boats. Groups Four and Five, assigned to Kristiansand and Oslo, did not have to sail so early. The idea was that all five groups would hit their objectives at more or less the same time.

One Allied officer at least believed that he knew what the Germans intended, even before the invasion forces set sail. He was Vice Admiral Sir Max Horton, commanding the Royal Navy's submarine flotillas. On his own initiative, he sent all available submarines – 12 in all – to lie off the German ports and patrol the sea routes to Norway. Throughout that day they saw many northward-bound cargo vessels pass before their periscopes, but because their orders were to attack only those ships recognizable as warships or troopships, they let them go.

Then, on the eighth, the Polish submarine *Orzel* torpedoed and sank the troop transport *Rio de Janeiro* off Lillesand, on the south coast of Norway. Norwegian fishermen rescued about 100 survivors, some of whom, interrogated by the military authorities, revealed that they had been on their way to Bergen "to protect Norway against English invaders."

The military authorities at once called for the full mobilization of Norway's small armed forces, and the mining of the approaches to the Noregian harbours. The pacifist Norwegian Government, fearful of provoking Nazi Germany even at this late hour, did nothing. And all the while, the enemy task groups were drawing closer to their objectives. Already, on the previous day, the units of Task Group One had been sighted by the crews of some RAF Coastal Command Blenheims, carrying out shipping searches from bases in Scotland. The Blenheims had attacked, but no hits had been obtained.

A few hours later units of the Home Fleet, including two battleships and several cruisers, sailed from Scapa Flow under their Commander-in-Chief, Admiral Sir Charles Forbes, with orders to intercept the enemy warships reported by the RAF. Even now, the belief still persisted that the Germans were breaking out into the North Atlantic, to prey on Britain's supply convoys. By the early hours of 8

April, fierce gales were lashing the Norwegian Sea. The ships of both sides plunged on in screaming winds and icy darkness, massive waves crashing over them and battering their superstructures.

One such wave plucked a seaman bodily from the deck of the battle-cruiser HMS *Renown* and hurled him overboard; an escorting destroyer, HMS *Glowworm*, was instructed to leave the main force and carry out a hopeless search for him. While engaged in this task, in a murky dawn, she sighted the warships of Task Group Two, bound for Trondheim. An enemy destroyer loomed up, her outline blurred by spray. *Glowworm* fired two salvoes at her before she was lost to sight in the heavy seas and fog. A few minutes later, *Glowworm* sighted a second destroyer and gave chase, the two warships exchanging shot for shot. The larger German vessel increased speed to try to shake off the dogged British destroyer but her bows ploughed under, forcing her to slow down again. *Glowworm* closed in, her skipper, Lieutenant Commander Roope, trying to get into position for a shot with torpedoes.

Some distance ahead, a great, dark shape burst from a fog-bank. For a few moments the men on *Glowworm*'s bridge were elated, believing the ship to be HMS *Renown*. Then a salvo of heavy shells tore into the British destroyer, setting her on fire. The newcomer to the battle was the *Admiral Hipper*. She forged towards the *Glowworm*, which turned away, belching clouds of smoke. The German cruiser lost sight of her and pursued her into the smokescreen, intent on delivering the *coup de grace*.

Suddenly, the destroyer came into view once more, her helm hard over, plunging headlong on a collision course with the *Hipper*. The cruiser tried to take avoiding action, but her response was too slow. *Glowworm* tore into the *Hipper*'s flank, shearing away over 100 feet of the cruiser's armour plating in a nightmare crescendo of rending metal. Recoiling from the collision she fell astern, ablaze and sinking.

There was a violent explosion, a mushroom of flame and smoke, and *Glowworm* disappeared.

Kapitän Heye, the *Hipper*'s commander, ordered his ship to heave to and search for survivors. His crew plucked 38 of them from the sea, shocked, frozen and smothered in oil, some of them badly injured. A 39th, Lieutenant Commander Roope, struggled weakly in the sea. German seamen threw him a line and he clutched at it, only to have it slip from his hands. He fell back, exhausted, and the waves closed over him.

So ended the first of many desperate, isolated naval actions that would be fought in these freezing waters in the days to come.

The day wore on and the weather steadily worsened. The main units of the Home Fleet under Admiral Forbes were still a long way from the scene of the action, although Forbes had sent the battlecruiser HMS *Repulse* and the cruiser HMS *Penelope* racing northwards with all speed to join HMS *Renown* and her destroyers, 500 miles away, playing an unwitting game of hide-and-seek with the Germans in squalls of ice and rain and appalling visibility.

There was still no indication as to where the enemy warships might be heading, but at ten minutes to seven that evening, 8 April, the Admiralty in London finally made up its mind about what was really happening, and a signal was flashed to the commander of the northernmost group of British warships – Vice Admiral William Whitworth, in HMS *Renown*. It was terse and to the point.

> 'Most immediate. The force under your orders is to concentrate on preventing any German force proceeding to Narvik.'

It was too late. Before midnight, the German invasion forces were already entering the dark fjords that led to their objectives.

Narvik, 9 April 1940: 06.15 hours

For several hours the destroyers had been nosing their way through the fog that enveloped Vestfjorden, the narrow waterway between the Lofoten Islands and the Norwegian mainland, their crews alert for British mines. The destroyers were crammed with the troops of the German Third Mountain Division, under General Dietl.

There were ten warships in all. As they slipped into Ofot Fjord, on the approach to Narvik, the German naval commander, *Kommodore* Friedrich

Bonte, detached seven destroyers: three to deal with the Norwegian forts said to be defending the Ramnes Narrows, and four to occupy the township of Elvegaard in Herjangs Fjord. The remaining three, with Bonte leading in the *Heidkamp*, the *Arnim* and *Thiele* close behind, sailed on to Narvik.

The harbour was crowded with the merchant ships of many nations, most of them ore carriers. At its entrance was the only obstacle Bonte's destroyer force had encountered so far: the Norwegian coastal defence vessel *Eidsvold*. She was ancient, dating back to 1900, but heavily armed with two 8-inch and six 6-inch guns – still no match for the destroyers' quick-firing 5-inch weapons and torpedoes.

Bonte, confident that she would not resist, sent an emissary to her skipper, Commander Willoch, demanding a free passage into the harbour. Willoch refused. Minutes later he was dead, together with most of his crew, their ship blasted by the *Heidkamp*'s torpedoes.

The explosions alerted the crew of the *Eidsvold*'s sister ship, the *Norge*. They tumbled to their stations in time to see the destroyer *Arnim* slipping alongside a jetty, her decks crowded with troops. The *Norge* managed to fire one salvo before she went to the bottom, shattered by torpedoes and shells. 50 of her crew struggled ashore.

There was no further resistance. The small Norwegian Army garrison in Narvik quickly surrendered and the German Mountain Troops fanned out through the town. The population, startled by the explosions and gunfire, came out into the streets to find German troops walking by, carrying placards that read in Norwegian: "Be calm. Take things easy. We have come to help you against the English." Bemused, uncomprehending, the people of Narvik went about their morning business.

On board the *Wilhelm Heidkamp*, *Kommodore* Bonte redeployed his destroyers, bringing others into Narvik. Then he went to his bunk to snatch a few hours' sleep. He had less than 24 hours left to live.

Early in the afternoon there came an unexpected break in the weather, and the *Luftwaffe* seized its opportunity. For nearly three hours, units of the Home Fleet operating off Bergen were attacked almost without pause by 41 Heinkels and 47 Junkers 88s. The battleship HMS *Rodney* took a direct hit from a 1,000-pound bomb, but escaped serious damage; the cruisers *Devonshire, Southampton* and *Glasgow* were also hit and damaged, and the destroyer *Gurkha* was sunk west of Stavanger.

While this action was in progress, a solitary Spitfire, its pilot also taking advantage of the unexpected break in the weather, droned high over Bergen harbour, its cameras clicking. Clusters of flak rose to challenge it from German warships, but they failed to reach the Spitfire's altitude. His job done, Wing Commander Royston set course for the Orkney Islands, racing against time and the weather front that was building rapidly over the Norwegian Sea.

Narvik, 10 April 1940: 04.30 hours

Kommodore Bonte slept for the second time since his arrival in Narvik, together with most of his crew. The previous day had been hectic, and in one sense frustrating. After landing their troops, all ten German destroyers should have been sailing back to Germany at high speed by nightfall; but before they could do so they needed fuel, and only one of the expected tankers had turned up. Bonte had therefore decided to delay the voyage home until the tenth, while his destroyers took it in turns to take on fuel.

Dawn was breaking; a white dawn, the snow that lay in drifts on the hillsides around the harbour blending with the lightening sky. The outlines of the hills, and of the ships in the harbour, were blurred by flurries of snow.

Death for *Kommodore* Bonte, and most of his crew, came without warning, its emissary a torpedo that tore through the *Heidkamp*'s plating and exploded in her after magazine. A great blast of flame and smoke burst high into the air, the echoes of the explosion reverberating round the hills. Burning debris hissed down into the freezing water, all that remained of the 2,400-ton vessel.

For Captain Warburton-Lee, RN, whose small force of five destroyers had been patrolling the entrance to Vestfjorden, it had been a long and lonely night. Somewhere up there in the darkness and the snow, beyond Ofot Fjord, were God knew how many enemy destroyers, and maybe submarines too. And he had been ordered into the unknown, to proceed to Narvik "... to make certain that no enemy troops land," in the words of the Admiralty signal, or if they had already landed "to sink or capture enemy ships and land forces if you think you can recapture Narvik from number of enemy present".

Detaching two of his ships – the *Hotspur* and *Hostile* – to search for and destroy enemy shore batteries, Warburton-Lee smashed on through the night at 20 knots towards Narvik in HMS *Hardy*, together with HMS *Hunter* and HMS *Havock*. Reaching the harbour, the sight of so many ships made the officers on *Hardy*'s bridge gasp. Warburton-Lee quickly recovered his composure.

"Well," he ordered, "get on with it!"

The torpedo that destroyed the *Heidkamp* was followed by six more, in quick succession. Two of them exploded on the flank of a second destroyer, the *Anton Schmitt*, and she went down in minutes. The other four struck merchant vessels, or missed their targets to explode against the rocky shore.

Hardy swung round in a wide circle, her 4.7-inch guns blazing. The other two destroyers, *Hunter* and *Havock*, came crashing into the harbour in their turn, adding to the carnage. Their shells punched into the *Hans Ludemann*, setting her ablaze, and then they turned on the *Diether von Roeder* like terriers, reducing her to a burning, shattered wreck that only just managed to reach the shore, where her captain beached her. Only one German destroyer escaped, and even then she was disabled, her engines damaged by the explosions of the torpedoes which sank the *Schmitt*.

At full speed, the three British destroyers sailed out of Narvik harbour. Rejoining the other two, they headed westwards down Ofot Fjord. It was 05.30 hours. Ahead of them, two more German destroyers, the *Georg Thiele* and *Berndt von Arnim*, alerted by frantic signals from Narvik, crept out of fogbound Ballangen Fjord into the British warships' path. Warburton-Lee's vessels were now being pursued by the three destroyers which *Kommodore* Bonte had stationed in Ofot Fjord, and were consequently trapped between two enemy forces. In the savage fight that ensued, HMS *Hardy* received the full weight of fire from the *Thiele* and *Arnim*. With her captain mortally wounded and her steering gear shattered, she grounded on some rocks 300 yards from shore. 170 men struggled to safety, taking Captain Warburton-Lee with them, strapped to a Carley Float. He died just as they dragged him from the water.

Lieutenant Commander de Villiers in HMS *Hunter* now led the British line. Raked by shells and burning, *Hunter* rapidly lost way, wallowing to a stop in the water. Close behind her, Lieutenant Commander Layman in HMS *Hotspur* gave urgent orders to take avoiding action, but at that moment a German shell cut the steering controls. With a terrific crash, *Hotspur*'s bow ripped into the helpless destroyer ahead of her.

Both destroyers now came under heavy fire. With shells bursting all around, Layman managed to make his way from the bridge to the after steering position. After much effort, he managed to extricate his badly damaged ship from the sinking *Hunter*. The other two British destroyers, *Havock* and *Hostile*, came to *Hotspur*'s rescue, engaging the *Thiele* and *Arnim* as the latter ran down the fjord in the opposite direction. The vessels disappeared into the murk, leaving the British warships free to continue their dash for the open sea.

Of *Hunter*'s crew of nearly 200, 50 men were rescued from the freezing waters.

It was not quite over. As the British destroyers headed seawards, they sighted a large German merchant ship, the *Rauenfels*, entering the fjord. Two shells compelled her crew to abandon ship; two more sent her sky-high in a shattering explosion that brought rocks tumbling in an avalanche from the surrounding cliffs. The Germans might still be in possession of Narvik, but their surviving destroyers could no longer depend on fresh supplies of ammunition with which to replenish their dwindling stocks.

The action had lasted less than two hours from start to finish. It had cost the Germans two destroyers sunk and three so badly damaged as to be unseaworthy, set against the British loss of two ships. Several hundred young men had been blown to pieces by shells or torpedoes, died screaming in flames, or gasped their last in icy blackness. It was only the beginning.

Chapter Twelve

The Orkney Islands, 10 April 1940: 04.15 hours

Armstrong's sojourn at Kinloss had been short-lived. Together with Royston, he had arrived after a gruelling flight through bad weather to find an urgent signal waiting. Both Spitfires were to deploy immediately to Hatston, in the Orkneys, to carry out operations in support of the Fleet Air Arm. Royston had ordered the third Spitfire to remain at Deanland, where its two pilots were to take it in turns to carry on the dangerous business of keeping a watch on the North German ports.

So, after snatching a bite to eat and a short rest, Royston and Armstrong had flown on to Hatston, near Kirkwall, from where both pilots had carried out reconnaissance sorties over the Bergen area on 9 April. Exhausted, they had tumbled into their beds and slept the sleep of the dead for several hours before being roused in the middle of the night and summoned to an urgent briefing. The photographs secured by Royston, their content confirmed by Armstrong's on the second sortie, revealed a target that was too good to miss.

The briefing room was crowded. There had been

no time for a proper breakfast, but plates laden with hot bacon sandwiches were passing around among the naval aircrews, taking the edge off their hunger, while a large urn on a trestle table supplied scalding hot tea. Royston and Armstrong helped themselves and sat down at the back of the room; although they had been asked to attend the briefing to help answer any questions that might arise, they had done their main part and this was now the Fleet Air Arm's "show".

Armstrong heard someone call his name from the other side of the room. Startled, he looked in that direction and saw a naval officer waving to him. It was Dickie Baird. He was about to go over and exchange a few words when there was a call for silence from the front and a lieutenant commander stepped up on to a low dais. He pulled a string, unfurling a white screen on the wall behind the dais, then nodded to a projectionist who had been busily setting up his equipment near the door, at the end of the aisle that ran between the rows of chairs.

"All set? Good. Let's have the lights down, please, and the first of the photographs."

The lights dimmed, and one of the photographs taken by Royston flashed up on the screen. It was a vertical shot, blown up several times, and centred perfectly in it was a warship.

"There she is, gentlemen," the naval officer said, "caught with her knickers down, thanks to our RAF colleagues back there." He nodded to Royston and Armstrong. "A very fine result, if I may say so."

There was a ripple of assent from the assembled aircrew.

"Those of you whose ship recognition is up to date will have identified her already," the lieutenant commander went on, tapping the image on the screen with a snooker cue. "She is the *Königsberg*, a light cruiser of around 6500 tons. That indispensable work of reference, *Jane's Fighting Ships*, assures us that she is armed with three triple turrets each mounting a trio of five-point-nine inch guns, and that she carries a total of fourteen light anti-aircraft weapons. The main point, though, is that she doesn't have much in the way of armour; her deck protection is only threequarters of an inch thick, which makes her highly vulnerable to dive-bombers. So, gentlemen, we are going to nip over to Bergen and sink her."

He raised his hand to still the murmur of excitement that greeted his remark and continued his briefing in quiet, clipped tones. One by one, the photographs brought back by Royston and Armstrong flashed up on the screen. The briefing officer drew the men's attention to one in particular, which revealed the warship at a slight angle and which had been blown up so far that it was blurred and grainy. It showed clear signs of battle damage to the cruiser's superstructure.

"You can see quite clearly that she's been hit," the naval officer said, "and that people are working flat out to patch her up." With his cue, he indicated small craft clustered alongside and what appeared to be working parties labouring in the vicinity of the damaged areas.

"I don't think the damage is too serious," the officer said, "so it is vital that we strike quickly. And by that, I mean that we must plan to arrive over the target at dawn in order to catch her before she has a chance to move and also to achieve maximum surprise. We don't yet know if the Germans have fighters in the Bergen area, but we must assume that they have. By the way, I should mention that Bergen harbour was attacked by the RAF last evening, but apparently they didn't hit anything."

"As usual," some wag commented, and there were a few chuckles. The briefing officer raised his hand again. "All right, let's not get too cocky. Remember it's all up to us now, and we don't want egg on our faces. So here's the plan. May we have the lights back on, please?"

The projectionist flicked a switch near the door, flooding the room with light again. The briefing officer blinked and cleared his throat.

"We have sixteen Skuas available for this operation, eleven from 803 Squadron and five from 800. They will fly in two waves, keeping sight of each other all the time. Accurate navigation is of paramount importance, so the most experienced Observer will fly in the leading aircraft. That's me, by the way." One or two hoots of derision came from the audience and the lieutenant commander lifted a corner of his mouth in a half-smile before continuing.

"Take-off will be at 05.10 hours; the weather should have cleared a bit by then." Outside it was dismal, with flurries of snow sweeping across the airfield. "Each aircraft will carry one 500-pound semi-armour-piercing bomb. We shall be operating at the limit of our range, so the course immediately after take-off is zero-five-zero degrees, which will lead us straight to the target area – with a bit of luck," he added, smiling at the earlier slur on his navigational ability.

"We shall climb to 12,000 feet and make landfall on the Norwegian coast at sixty degrees, nine minutes north. Strict radio silence will be maintained during the sea crossing and on the run-up to the target unless enemy fighters are sighted. If the weather remains as forecast the first group should arrive over the target at around 07.15. Our weather people are predicting a thin layer of cloud at 8–10,000 feet in the Bergen area, with good visibility underneath, so we should have no trouble in locating the cruiser. Aircraft will attack in line astern. . . ."

Royston and Armstrong listened intently as the lieutenant commander went on to complete his briefing. Afterwards, one or two of the aircrew came up to them and asked, rather shyly, what it was like over the target; whether they had experienced any flak and so forth. Realizing that it was the first mission of its kind that these young naval airmen had ever flown for real, the RAF pilots did their best to reassure them.

"You don't need to worry overmuch about flak," Royston lied. "It always looks much worse than it actually is, and it's mostly inaccurate. Fighters are much more of a worry, but neither Flight Lieutenant

Armstrong nor myself saw any in the vicinity. You'll be OK."

"I suppose you could class that as a load of bull-shit, Ken?" Dickie Baird said quietly to Armstrong a few minutes later as he sipped a last mug of tea before going off to make his final preparations for the flight. "I remember Wilhelmshaven only too well." Baird had just met Royston for the first time.

"Yes," Armstrong agreed, "but this show ought to be a bit different. The Huns probably haven't had time to set up shore batteries, and you'll be above the light stuff from the cruiser until you are well into your dive. You'll be going like the clappers then, so they won't hit you. Only the good die young, anyway," he added with a grin.

"Let's hope you're right," Baird said. He glanced at his wristwatch. "Well, time to be off. See you later." He turned and left the building, followed by his Observer, who had waited behind for him.

Half an hour later, Hatston throbbed with sound as 16 Bristol Perseus radial engines burst into life. One by one, the bomb-laden Skuas lifted from the ground. Some cleared the end of the short runway by only a matter of feet, but at last all 16 were safely airborne. Forming up overhead, they climbed laboriously into the darkened north-eastern sky. Ahead of them lay 300 miles of icy sea, and Norway.

For nearly two hours they droned steadily on. Ahead of them now, the pink and green flush of dawn began to spread across the sky. At seven o'clock, a dark, broken line rose out of the horizon; the black cliffs of the Norwegian coast. A bright sun burst out over the mountains beyond and suddenly the pilots made out the entrance to Bergen Fjord. After flying 300 miles through the night, they had made landfall in exactly the right place and within seconds of their estimated time of arrival.

As the aircraft swept up the fjord, with Bergen itself becoming visible out of the thin morning haze, Dickie Baird, who was part of the second group, saw the leading wave go into line astern as it by-passed the town and headed for the mountains. A minute later his own group adopted a similar formation, so that all 16 aircraft resembled a long snake, weaving its way through the cold dawn sky. To the east of the town the head of the snake turned, placing the sun behind it, and began its descent through the thin cloud layer that partially obscured the town and its harbour.

As Baird turned and descended through the cloud layer in his turn he spotted the cruiser, moored hard up against the Skoltegrund Mole. Ahead and below, the first wave was starting its attack, the Skuas seeming to falter momentarily in mid-air as the pilots lowered their big flaps. As a dive-bomber, the Skua was unsurpassed. It could dive vertically at near-constant speed, held back by its huge flap area, and the pilot's visibility was excellent.

"Stand by," Baird told his Observer. "We're going down now."

Bombs were already exploding around the *Königsberg* as Baird began his dive, taking careful aim on the warship. He increased the angle of the dive until the Skua was plummeting towards its objective at nearly 70 degrees. He held the aircraft rock-steady, watching the long shape of the cruiser, partly hidden now by drifting smoke, loom up in his sights. At 4000 feet the first bursts of flak came up, the blotchy yellow smoke whipping past the Skua. At 2000 feet Baird pressed the bomb release and the 500-pounder dropped away, curving down to explode near the warship's stern in a geyser of foam. As he came out of his dive and pulled a hard turn to starboard he saw the cruiser's decks erupt in smoke and flame as other Skuas came down on her.

The aircraft weaved their way out of the harbour at low level, heading for the comparative safety of the sea. Astern of them, the cruiser was finished. She had sustained three direct hits, one amidships between her funnels, one on the port quarter and one on "A" turret. Two more exploded between the ship and the mole, tearing gaping holes in her side. Five pulverized the mole itself, and the rest were all near misses. An enormous column of flame burst from the stricken warship and she began to list heavily. Five minutes later, a thin plume of brown smoke speared into the air as her magazines went up and she broke in half, sinking in a cloud of steam.

Skimming the water, the Skuas sped through a smoky spider's web of tracer from small arms on the shore. One of the aircraft suddenly dived into the harbour at full throttle, disintegrating in a cloud of wreckage. The others formed up over Lyso Island and set course for home. The first of them landed at Hatston at 09.45, after a flight that had lasted four and a half hours. The engines of three aircraft spluttered and died as they turned clear of the runway; their fuel tanks were empty.

Baird and his observer climbed wearily from the Skua's long cockpit and slid off the wing onto the slushy ground, pulling off their flying helmets. Their hair, wet with sweat, started to freeze in the icy wind as they walked towards their dispersal hut. It felt good.

Stavanger airfield, Norway,
afternoon, 10 April 1940

"*Verdammt*!" The base commander at Stavanger aerodrome was in a towering rage. He had spent most of the afternoon being harangued by a succession of senior naval officers, his ears were burning, and he was humiliated. Before him, on the carpet, stood the commanding officer of the Me 110 squadron whose responsibility it was to provide air cover for the German naval unit operating off south-west Norway. Well, the squadron hadn't done much by way of defending the *Königsberg*; by the time the first Me 110s had arrived overhead, the cruiser was already at the bottom of Bergen harbour.

"If I may explain to the *Herr Oberst*— " the squadron commander began. The base commander cut him short, rising from his seat and stamping over to the window.

"Explanations!" he snapped. "Excuses! I've had them all. The fact remains that we have failed in our duty, and it must not be allowed to happen again. We know the problems, and the biggest problem of all lies with those infernal reconnaissance Spitfires. Thanks to them, the Tommies know every move we make. We know they are there and what they are doing, but we can't get at them. Your Me 110s do not have the rate of climb to reach their altitude in time to intercept them, and even if you did they can easily out-run you."

He returned to his desk and sat down again, glaring at his subordinate. "It's not your fault," he admitted grudgingly. "I'm aware of that. We have no warning system in place as yet, and you can't be expected to perform miracles. It would be out of the question to mount continuous patrols; the English are not as punctual as we Germans, and are inconsiderate enough to make their reconnaissance flights at different times of the day." He permitted himself a smile in recognition of his ponderous attempt at wit.

A telephone on the base commander's desk top shrilled. He picked the instrument up and grunted into it. Then he beamed, replaced the receiver and rubbed his hands together.

"Excellent! Better late than never, as the English say. It seems that my antidote to the Spitfires is on its way here at this very moment. Come – let us go outside and welcome it."

The "antidote to the Spitfires" was not ecstatically happy. From the cockpit of his Messerschmitt 109, Hans Lehmann, newly promoted to the rank of *Hauptmann*, stared moodily at the rugged landscape of southern Norway as it unfolded beneath him. This would, his superiors had told him, be only a temporary detachment; it appeared that the Naval authorities in Norway were having trouble with high-flying reconnaissance aircraft. All he had to do was to deal with them, and then he could return to Jever.

Lehmann derived some small comfort from the fact that he was not alone. He was accompanied by his trusty wingman, Falcke, also recently promoted with the rank of *Feldwebel*, whose 109 rose and fell gently on the currents of air a couple of hundred metres away.

The order for the move had come only hours earlier, and had been assigned the highest priority. Lehmann fully realized why he had been picked; he and Falcke, together with other experienced pilots at Jever, had often operated against the high-flying reconnaissance Spitfires that had cruised over Wilhelmshaven and Bremen during the last few weeks, and so they were experienced in this kind of work. The problem was that they had so far failed to shoot one down, a fact that appeared to have escaped the notice of those who had organized this trip.

Because of the 109's relatively short range, Lehmann had decided to stop off at the recently-occupied Danish airfield of Aalborg in order to refuel before continuing on to Stavanger. He had a pilot's natural mistrust of weather forecasters, and topping up in this way would mean that they would have sufficient fuel to return to Jever in the event of running into bad weather *en route*.

As it turned out, Lehmann need not have worried. The sun shone brightly throughout the flight, there was only scattered cloud, and the airfield at Stavanger was readily identified when it appeared up ahead. In a way, Lehmann was rather sorry when the wheels of his fighter kissed the ground; he suddenly realized that he had been enjoying himself, and he had to admit that the Norwegian scenery was breathtakingly beautiful.

When the base commander, no less, turned out to meet him, accompanied by the commander of the resident Me 110 squadron, Lehmann felt positively important. The bubble burst dramatically when, as they were walking to the *Oberst's* staff car, the latter suddenly stopped dead in his tracks and stared up into the clear sky, his mouth open. Then he gave vent to a string of curses and shook his fist at a thin vapour trail that was describing a perfect arc high overhead.

Strapped in his Spitfire's cockpit, Ken Armstrong, who was making a last-light reconnaissance of the area, had no idea of all the fuss he was creating 25,000 feet below.

Chapter Thirteen

From the window of his large office on the top floor of the Bank of Norway, Nicolas Rygg, the bank's president, had a fine view over the port of Oslo. The port was crowded with ships, the majority of them German.

Rygg, an athletic man in his sixties, scratched his grey, crewcut hair. He had yet to come to terms with the fact that his country had been invaded, that German forces had occupied most of the key points in the south and that the small Norwegian Army was being remorselessly overwhelmed. Rygg already knew a great deal about the pattern the invasion was taking, because Norwegians were still in control of the telephone system and he had been receiving a steady flow of information for the past 24 hours.

Rygg was desperately weary, but he knew that there was no time for sleep. The weight of responsibility that lay on his shoulders was enormous. In the bank's vaults lay 1542 crates containing 50 tons of gold, the whole lot worth 55 million dollars. It was the lifeblood of the Norwegian economy – and somehow, Rygg had to get it out of Oslo under the very noses of the Germans.

At that moment, every member of the bank's staff capable of walking was heading towards the building in response to Rygg's summons, even though it was half-past six in the morning. Moving the gold from the vaults would not present a problem; acquiring the necessary transport, on the other hand, would. The Transport Minister had already informed him that no trucks were available.

There was only one thing for it. As soon as the senior members of his staff began to arrive, Rygg sent them out into the street to flag down any passing truck they could find. Within half an hour they had found six, one of which was a milk delivery waggon, and the loading began. By eight-thirty the first was on its way, accompanied by an armed guard, heading northwards to join the road that went to Lillehammer.

Two hours later, in the street that ran in front of the bank, a convoy of vehicles of every shape and size waited their turn to load up with the precious metal. All the while, the radio news bulletins grew more and more alarming. German forces had occupied all of Norway's major seaports. Rygg reasoned that enemy troops would be in the streets of Oslo at any moment, now that they had completed their task of overcoming the city's outer defences. There were already rumours that government buildings were in enemy hands; it was a stroke of luck that the Germans had not yet descended on the bank.

Desperately, Rygg – himself pouring with sweat as he took a hand in the loading operation – tried to speed up the work. At 12.15, the last lorry moved off with Rygg on board. His final act was to hand over the keys of the bank to one the employees who had elected to stay behind.

Three-quarters of an hours later, Major Neef, an officer on General von Falkenhorst's headquarters staff, arrived at the bank with an armed escort. He told the senior member of staff that he had come to place the nation's gold reserves under the protection of the Führer. The employee obligingly showed him the vaults. They were empty.

By nightfall, Rygg's convoy of 50 vehicles had reached Lillehammer, where the gold was offloaded and placed in a secret vault in the town's small bank. The vehicles, together with their obliging drivers, returned to Oslo.

At Lillehammer, Rygg constantly monitored the rapidly deteriorating political and military situation. To his dismay, he learned that Vidkun Quisling, a pro-Nazi member of the Norwegian Government, had been appointed Head of State in place of King Haakon, who had sought refuge in the north of the country. Also, the Germans were making heavy attacks on the Norwegian forces grouped between Oslo and Lillehammer, their intention being to break through and link up with the seaborne units that had gone ashore at Trondheim.

It was fortunate that General Otto Ruge, newly appointed as the Norwegian Commander-in-Chief, had moved his headquarters to Lillehammer from Oslo at the first warning of an impending invasion. Nicolas Rygg went to see him, and was told that an Anglo-French force was to be landed in Norway, its initial objective to recapture Trondheim. That, thought Rygg, would be the best way out. If the Allies retook Trondheim, he would be able to ship the gold out to England. But first, he had to get the consignment to the port.

"How long do you think you can hold on here?" he asked the General.

"A week at the outside," Ruge told him, "if the Allies don't intervene in the meantime." In his heart of hearts, Ruge knew that the motley force of 12,000 men under his command would be incapable of resisting the enemy onslaught for more than two or three days. The *Luftwaffe* was already operating in strength over Lillehammer, and there was nothing to oppose it. The Norwegian Air Force had ceased to exist.

For Nicolas Rygg, there was more bad news to come. In the afternoon of 12 April an exhausted courier arrived in Lillehammer. Rygg recognized him as one of the bank's messengers. The man told him that the Germans knew the whereabouts of the gold, thanks to the careless gossip of a cleaning woman.

"So," Rygg mused, "those German planes must be watching for any sign of movement. The noose is tightening about our necks, General."

Ruge agreed. "Moreover, we are vulnerable to an airborne assault here." He tapped a map that lay on the table in front of him. "The Germans wouldn't risk dropping paratroops directly on to the town, and the area roundabout is too mountainous. But here, just a few kilometres to the north, is Lake

Nijos, and it is still frozen over. They might drop men there, and then march on Lillehammer."

Ruge bent over his map again. "It is high time to move your gold, I think. See here." His finger traced a line across the map from Lillehammer to the coast. "This railway line runs from here to Aandalsnes, south of Trondheim. As you know, that's a small port, which is probably why the Germans thought it too insignificant to occupy. As a consequence it is still in our hands."

He looked at Rygg and smiled. "We'll beat them yet. There's a train in one of the sidings here. I'll have it requisitioned. I will also round up some of the local people to transport the gold from the bank to the station. We'll do it tonight. I'll declare a curfew, just in case there are any prying eyes about. Oh, and there's just one other thing. You've done your bit, Rygg. From now on, this is a military operation. Once the gold is on the move again, I will get off a signal to our English friends to let them know where we are taking it, and to arrange for a ship to transport it to England.

It was purely by chance that Ruge hit hit upon Aandalsnes as the gold's destination. He was unaware, as yet, that the port already featured prominently in the Allies' plans for the reconquest of Norway.

Wing Commander Royston had been forced to look up Aandalsnes on the map, never having heard of the place before. He found it at length, at the head of Molde Fjord, and wondered what conditions there would be like. Pretty bloody awful, he suspected. Well, he would soon find out for himself. Detach one Spitfire to Aandalsnes, with appropriate photographic processing equipment, in support of Allied Expeditionary Force operations, his orders had stated. It was only fair that he should volunteer for the job himself, leaving Armstrong behind to cope with things at home.

Before that, though, there was yet another routine reconnaisance to be flown over the Bergen area. He was becoming used to this run; in fact, almost complacent about it. His aircraft was still inside the contrail layer as it crossed the Norwegian coast, and dragging a streamer of white vapour that must be visible over a vast area, but it didn't seem to matter. He yawned into his oxygen mask, even though he didn't feel tired. Quite the reverse; he felt a kind of light-headedness, almost a type of elation.

He never thought of checking the tiny meter that showed how efficiently the oxygen was flowing from its cylinder to the mask strapped to his face. Had he done so, he would have seen that it was drastically reduced. There was something wrong with the valve. Slowly and relentlessly, Horace Royston's lungs were being starved of the precious gas. The Spitfire flew on, and as it did so little erratic kinks appeared in its contrail as, without knowing it, Royston made movements on the stick that caused the aircraft to weave from side to side.

A few thousand feet below, two more contrails were beginning to form as hot engine gases turned into freezing vapour.

"This time we have him, Falcke!" Lehmann did not utter the words out loud. His eyes were on the little dark cross at the head of the vapour trail above.

This time, there had been plenty of warning of the Spitfire's approach, signalled by a picket ship stationed several miles offshore. Two previous attempts to intercept the intruding, high-flying Spitfires had ended in failure, but this time, there would be no mistake.

Lehmann had no need to glance back to see if Falcke was in his accustomed position. He knew that his wingman would be there. Keeping his eyes on the Spitfire, which was growing larger in his windscreen, Lehmann was puzzled; normally, the Tommies had made their turn before now and were heading back over the harbour, but this one was flying straight on. The German noticed that the Englishman seemed to be flying erratically, too.

The Spitfire now filled the whole of Lehmann's windscreen. He noticed that the white paint on its undersurfaces was streaked with oil. He made a slight adjustment to his gunsight, and fired. The vibration from his guns caused the image of the aircraft in front to tremble.

Royston barely had time to register the impact of the Me 109's cannon shells before his aircraft went violently out of control. Sky, mountains and the distant sea gyrated wildly around him in succession as his aircraft dropped into a spin. As it fell, his head began to clear and he realized with a shock what must have happened to him.

He allowed the Spitfire to spin through several thousand feet, into air that was richer in oxygen, before taking the appropriate recovery action – stick forward to unstall the wings, hard rudder in the opposite direction to the spin's rotation. The aircraft came out of the spin in a screaming vertical dive, its nose pointing towards the fjord that was still far below. Relief swept over Royston with the knowledge that the controls were still functioning.

He looked back, and saw two Me 109s on his tail, closing rapidly. He knew that the Messerschmitt could out-dive the Spitfire, and that his only hope was to out-manoeuvre his pursuers.

Behind him, braced in his cockpit, grasping the control column with both hands, Lehmann doggedly clung to the Spitfire which had suddenly begun to twist and turn wildly. He fired again and his target aircraft began to trail smoke, which quickly became denser. The Spitfire levelled out and went into a steep climb; the manoeuvre took Lehmann by surprise and he overshot.

It didn't matter. Turning steeply, he saw that the Spitfire was being attacked by Falcke. Flames burst from it, and debris broke away. The aircraft became a glowing ball, trailing a thick banner of black smoke as it hurtled towards the fjord.

A dark shape parted from it, turning slowly end over end, attached to the falling aircraft as though by an invisible thread. Then it began to fall behind, and seconds later it began to trail a streamer of parachute silk that quickly blossomed into a white canopy.

'Well done, Falcke! You can claim that one!"

Even as Lehmann shouted his congratulations over the radio, he saw the doomed Spitfire plunge into the fjord, its grave marked by a spreading circle of foam and a cloud of smoke that began to drift slowly away on the wind.

Royston, who had been fished out of the fjord by a German patrol boat, was brought to Stavanger that evening. Both his hands were heavily bandaged and there were slight burns to his face, but whatever pain he felt was soon dispelled by a considerable quantity of brandy which his *Luftwaffe* hosts poured into him. They entertained him to dinner, before he was taken away on the first stage of his journey to a prisoner-of-war camp, and he showed no embarrassment at all over the fact that one of the German officers had to feed him because he could not handle a knife and fork. Considering the circumstances, it was a good-natured occasion. But if anyone had hoped that the brandy might loosen Royston's tongue, they were disillusioned.

The Norwegian Sea, 15 April 1940: dawn

For the RAF pilots on board the aircraft carrier HMS *Glorious*, heading for Aandalsnes with their Gloster Gladiator fighter biplanes, the last couple of days had been far from pleasant. Quite apart from the seasickness that affected a number of them, the carrier and her escorts, because of the threat posed by enemy submarines, had followed a zig-zag track and there had been several alarms which, fortunately, had turned out to be false. There had been only one bright spot during the voyage; late on 14 April the ship's captain had broadcast over the PA system the contents of a signal he had just received. That afternoon a force of British destroyers, supported by the battleship HMS *Warspite*, had sailed into Narvik and, with guns and torpedoes, finished off the job begun by the gallant Warburton-Lee a few days earlier. The German Navy now had ten fewer destroyers.

The pilots had been briefed on their forthcoming task. It was to provide air cover over the port of Aandalsnes and, if required, support for the ground forces that were already landing there. The prospect of action sounded promising; what was less so was the news that they would be operating from the surface of a frozen lake.

As he sat in the cockpit of his Gladiator on the carrier's deck in the icy dawn, each pilot was conscious that ahead of him lay a flight of 150 miles over nothing but sea, with only the reliability of the fighter's Bristol Mercury engine standing between him and a miserable death. HMS *Glorious* was steaming into wind at close to her maximum speed of 30 knots, and each aircraft had to be held down by a pair of naval ratings, heavily muffled and bent forward against the Arctic blast that howled down the carrier's deck.

None of the pilots had ever taken off from an aircraft carrier before, nor did they have experience of long flights over water. For that reason, each flight of three aircraft was led by a Blackburn Skua, whose crew would take care of the navigation.

A "batsman" in a yellow jacket marshalled each aircraft into position on the deck centreline. The pilot opened his throttles fully, holding the stick back. The ratings thankfully let go of the wingtips and vanished astern at a crouching run. The batsman, his legs set wide apart, his body braced with effortless experience against the heave of the slippery deck, turned sideways and made a sweeping motion. The pilot released the brakes and eased the stick forward a little. The Gladiator's tail came up and suddenly the pilot could see ahead along the deck, past the big engine cowling. Then, amazingly quickly, he was airborne and climbing away to join the others.

All 16 Gladiators and their Fleet Air Arm shepherds reached the Norwegian coast without incident. The Skua leading each flight waggled its wings and changed course a little to the south-east in order to stay well clear of Trondheim, heading inland and descending. The aircraft were sliding down into the middle of a bowl of mountains, their flanks ridged with dense pine woods that jutted up through the snow.

Ahead, the flat expanse of the frozen lake formed the bottom of the bowl. A strip across the surface of the lake had been cleared of snow, making an improvised runway, and taxi strips led from it to hidden places among the pines that ringed the lake.

Apart from the surface being a little bumpy the pilots found no difficulty in landing, although while taxying they had to be careful when using their brakes, otherwise the aircraft had a tendency to slide on the ice. They taxied across the lake to the fringe of pines. Figures emerged from the trees; men in baggy trousers and what appeared to be sheepskin coats. They wore odd-looking helmets. One of them came out to meet each aircraft and held up his arms as a signal to stop. The pilots did so, their engines still running. More men came out from the pines, groups of them seizing each aircraft, swinging it round and pushing it tail-first into little individual clearings that had been carved out.

An aircraft already stood in one such clearing. It was a French-built Mureaux 117 observation aircraft, recently flown to Aandalsnes across the North Sea.

Its pilot, who had been supervising some work on the aircraft's engine, watched the new arrivals with interest. He, unlike, the Mureaux, was not French. His name was Stanislaw Kalinski.

Chapter Fourteen

It had been a long and difficult road from the embattled skies over Warsaw to a frozen lake in Norway. Kalinski still found it hard to believe that not much more than six months had elapsed since he and his surviving comrades had escaped from Romania, where the authorities had interned them as soon as they learned of Poland's collapse. Their escape had been engineered by some members of a French military mission in Bucharest – exactly how, Kalinski had no idea, although he suspected that bribery had come into the picture – and it was on board a French freighter that they had sailed from the port of Constanta. A fortnight later, after calling at one or two ports in North Africa, they had arrived in France. There, within a few weeks, a Polish Government in Exile had been set up, and one of its first acts had been to form a new Polish military aviation structure under the command of General Sikorsky.

Kalinski, naturally, had wanted to be assigned to fighters; but after a month of going over old ground at a fighter instruction school at Etampes, where he had discovered that he knew far more than his instructors – and with no prospect of a Polish fighter squadron yet in sight – he had had enough. When the call came for volunteers to serve with an air observation squadron that was being formed to support an infantry brigade consisting of Polish troops who had also managed to escape from their enslaved homeland, he had seized his opportunity.

In many respects, the Mureaux aircraft that equipped the observation squadron, with its high parasol-type wing, resembled the PZLs that Kalinski had flown in Poland, although it trundled along at a much more sedate speed under the power of its 650 hp Hispano-Suiza engine. The view from the pilot's cockpit, which was open to the weather, was awful, but the observer in the rear cockpit had a good field of vision. He was armed with a 7.5 mm machine-gun, and the pilot controlled a similar weapon that fired through the propeller shaft. By the outbreak of war the Mureaux was obsolete, and it was being replaced by more up-to-date types in the French observation squadrons, whose weary cast-offs were assigned to the Poles.

The unit to which Kalinski was assigned was called the Polish Highland Mountain Brigade. Under French command, it formed part of the Allied Norwegian Expeditionary Force. Only one battalion had been sent to Aandalsnes, together with a British infantry brigade; the bulk of the Polish force was earmarked for a landing at Narvik.

Kalinski and his observer had flown the Mureaux across the English Channel and then proceeded in "hops" to the Orkneys, from where they had made the long oversea crossing to Aandalsnes, arriving at about the same time as the troops. The trip had not worried the Pole, for the Mureaux had a 600-mile range and its engine was reliable. Kalinski's two mechanics had crossed over with the main force; giving the aircraft a thorough overhaul before operations began in earnest was their first task.

It was with considerable envy that Kalinski, on the morning of 16 April, watched a sleek, low-wing monoplane winging towards the lake. It touched down flawlessly and was marshalled into a forest clearing close to the place where his own aircraft was concealed. It was the first Spitfire he had seen, and he wandered over to it, filled with curiosity.

Armstrong clambered stiffly from the cockpit and slid off the wing, stretching and flexing his aching leg muscles. He nodded amiably at the man who approached and stuck out a hand, introducing himself. Kalinski gave a little bow and did likewise. Armstrong raised an eyebrow.

"Polish? I didn't know there were any Poles here. Oh, hell, I don't suppose you understand a word I'm saying."

Kalinksi looked a little put out. "On the contrary. You will find that my English is quite passable. I elected to study the language at officer cadet school; most of the others took a course in French."

Armstrong grinned. "Sorry, old chap." He looked around. "Things seem pretty chaotic here, or am I wrong?"

It was Kalinski's turn to grin. "Chaotic would be an understatement. But the English squadron arrived only yesterday, and they have been flying defensive patrols from the start. There has not been much time for – how do you say it – works of administration."

Armstrong reflected briefly that he had not had much time to prepare himself for this deployment to Norway; but, when Royston had failed to return from his sortie to Bergen, his subordinate had naturally stepped in to carry out the operation. Armstrong could not bring himself to believe that the Wing Commander was gone; somehow, he was left with a strong gut feeling that Royston would show up again, some day.

The RAF airman who had marshalled Armstrong's aircraft into its dispersal, and who had temporarily disappeared while the pilot was unstrapping himself, returned with two companions.

"Your ground crew, sir," he explained. "They'll be looking after you all the time."

Well, Armstrong thought, at least somebody knew I was coming, which is a start. He exchanged a few words with the men, telling them to have the aircraft refuelled. One of them, who had been eyeing the Spitfire, had a puzzled expression on his face. Armstrong noticed it, and asked what was the matter.

"I . . . I was just wondering where the guns are, sir," the man replied hesitantly, as though fearful of making a fool of himself. Armstrong chuckled.

"Don't worry about that – there aren't any. It's a photo-reconnaissance aircraft. Incidentally, does anybody know where my photographic processing facilities have been set up?"

They shook their heads, mystified. All they knew was that they had been told to expect an incoming Spitfire. "Maybe they'll know in the headquarters building, sir," one of the men said. He indicated a solid-looking log farmhouse that stood by the lakeside about half a mile away.

Armstrong nodded. "Right. I'll take a look. It's shanks's pony, I suppose."

The airman grinned. "Afraid so, sir. Not so much as a bike to spare around here."

Kalinksi joined him as he set off to walk to the farmhouse, saying that he had to report in to see if any orders had come through for him. As they trudged on, a pair of Gladiators took off from the airstrip with a crackling roar, the slipstream from their engines kicking up a trail of powdery snow. As soon as they were airborne they went into a climbing turn, heading for the port. Kalinski told Armstrong that two Gladiators were on patrol over Aandalsnes at all times, one pair relieving the other. Armstrong wondered why he hadn't been intercepted as he flew inland; his route had taken him directly across the town.

The farmhouse was deserted apart from the farmer's wife, who was cooking a meal, and an army sergeant who was the duty NCO. He had no idea what had become of the rest of Armstrong's team either, but he thought that "the Colonel" might know something about it. He was expected back shortly. In the meantime, would Armstrong like something to eat?

Armstrong confessed that he was famished, and

in what seemed only seconds the farmer's wife had provided him with a bowl of steaming porridge, followed by fish and black bread, the whole washed down by a mug of coffee. The pilot had just cleaned his plate when "the Colonel" arrived.

Colonel Jack Gough of the Sherwood Foresters, it appeared, was in charge of pretty well everything at the lake – the name of which, Armstrong learned, was Lesjaskog – except the actual flying operations.

"Oh, yes," he told Armstrong, "I know where your photographic people have got to. Some clot put them in with the landing force that has gone ashore at Namsos, north of Trondheim. There isn't a hope in hell of getting them down here, I'm afraid, and there isn't much point in your going up there. But don't worry – there's plenty for you to do, believe me. For a start, I want you to go out and find a train for me."

Armstrong looked startled. "A train?"

Gough nodded, placing his cap and swagger stick on a roughly-hewn pinewood table. "Yes. Come over here and have a look."

He took Armstrong by the elbow and led him to a large map of southern Norway that was pinned to the wall. First of all, he indicated the railway line that ran through the mountains from Lillehammer to Aandalsnes.

"It's somewhere on this stretch of track," he explained. "The distance is about 150 miles and the wretched thing set off a couple of days ago, so it should have got here by now. It hasn't, though, and we are very concerned about it. It's a very important train, you see."

Kalinski came forward, a mug of coffee in his hand. "Perhaps I can be of assistance, Colonel?"

Gough nodded. "Most certainly, Captain. You have my full authority. It will be some time yet before our forces here are sufficiently strong to begin the advance on Trondheim. You will not be needed until then."

"May I ask why this train is so important, sir?" Armstrong asked.

"You may, but I'm afraid I can't tell you. Not yet, anyway. I can say, though, that if the Germans get their hands on it it will boost their war effort considerably. We must prevent that from happening, at all costs."

"How do we know that they haven't captured it already?" Armstrong wanted to know.

Gough referred to the map again. "Because their forces are nowhere near the railway line as yet," he explained. "They are still pushing northwards from Oslo. We know exactly where they are, because the Norwegians still control the telephone system and if the Germans appear in a town or village the local postmaster simply puts in a call to the next one up the road. Our intelligence sources are pretty good in that respect. Also, the Germans aren't having it all their own way, even though they have seized five out of six Norwegian divisional headquarters and practically paralyzed the army. It seems that the Norwegians are organizing themselves into fighting units and are opposing the enemy advance; the Norwegian commander in the area, General Ruge, is trying to set up a defensive line anchored on

Lillehammer, where he will hold on until we get to him."

Kalinski, who had first-hand experience of the speed with which the Germans were capable of breaking through defensive lines, thought that Gough was overly optimistic, but said nothing.

A sudden roar of engines low overhead made them all jump. The farmer's wife screamed and dropped a pan. The clatter it made was followed by a terrific thump from somewhere outside.

Kalinski led the rush out of the building. A column of smoke was beginning to rise from the lake shore a mile or so away. Overhead a Gladiator turned, its engine roaring. The pilot waggled his wings and then circled the lake before approaching to land.

"He's got a Jerry!" Gough said excitedly. "Come on – everyone into my car!"

They piled into the vehicle, which Gough had somehow acquired for use as his personal transport, and went skidding off across the lake towards the column of smoke, now shot with flames at its base. By the time they reached the enemy bomber, a Heinkel 111, it was blazing fiercely. The Heinkel had landed flat on its belly just short of the trees and was crushed. Only the tail fin and rudder, bearing a white-edged black swastika on bottle-green camouflage, remained intact. The whole forward part of the crumpled fuselage, and the wings – except for the outer portions – were being consumed by the flames.

"I say," Gough remarked, "what if the blighter's got bombs on board, and they go off?"

"I think they would have gone off by now," Armstrong reassured him. "I think this chap was on a long-range recce, so he'd be carrying a full fuel load rather than bombs. His guns will have been armed, though, so we'd better watch out for exploding ammunition. I suggest we keep well clear."

They all retreated a few paces until they were at a respectful distance from the wreck. Even so, the stench of the burning Heinkel still assailed their nostrils; it gave off a strange, sickly smell, something between burnt toast and milk spilt on a hot stove. Armstrong had an unpleasant vision of the German crew's remains, charring in the flames, but he knew that it was the magnesium used in the alloy of the Heinkel's construction that produced the stink. However, the knowledge that what was left of the German crew was in there somewhere gave them all cause for thought, and it was not long before they turned away.

"Well," Gough remarked as he drove them back to the farmhouse, "we got that one, but there'll be others, and doubtless they *will* be carrying bombs. It won't take much to put paid to the ice on the lake – there are signs of it thawing already. And my airfield defences, apart from the RAF fighters, of course, consist of exactly two machine-guns. It isn't exactly an encouraging picture."

Armstrong was forced to agree with him, especially after one of the mechanics assigned to look after his Spitfire reported to him with the news that there was no chance of obtaining any fuel until the following morning. The supplies already at the lake were jealously hoarded for use by the Gladiator squadron, and reserves had to be brought up from Aandalsnes.

Being in a state of enforced idleness, Armstrong took the opportunity of learning more of the situation at Aandalsnes. The Poles, he discovered, had the task of defending the lake from which the Gladiators were operating. The lake had been deliberately chosen not because Aandalsnes lacked an airstrip – in fact there was one, although it was very primitive – but because it lay about 20 miles south-east of the town, which meant that the Gladiators would have more time in which to intercept enemy bombers approaching from that direction, intent on bombing the harbour.

The main task on the ground was to be undertaken by the British 148th Infantry Brigade, which, with only two battalions, was badly under strength. Part of it was to move south-east along the railway line – the same line as the one along which the mysterious train was said to be travelling – and secure the town of Dombaas, while the remainder took offensive action against the Germans occupying Trondheim. Colonel Gough also informed Armstrong that a force of about 700 sailors and Royal Marines would be landing at Aandalsnes that night, bringing some naval artillery and anti-aircraft guns with them; their task would be to defend the town and harbour and if necessary provide reinforcements for the troops on the railway line to Dombaas.

That was as much as Armstrong knew. Had he been aware of the true situation, he would have been a good deal more gloomy than was the case. The entire Allied Norwegian Expedition was fraught with ill-luck. For one thing, the officer appointed to command the forces that were to retake Trondheim collapsed and died of a stroke only hours after being informed of his appointment; for another, the aircraft carrying his successor to Scapa Flow crashed on landing and the replacement general was injured, together with most of his staff. By the time a third commander had been appointed, the tactical picture had changed substantially.

The officer who eventually took command of the Aandalsnes force, now known as Sickleforce, was Major General Paget. His orders were to co-operate with the Norwegian Army in blocking the northward advance of the German Army, at the same time protecting his left flank and rear against a possible attack by the enemy forces in Trondheim, and from paratroop detachments on his lines of communication. In practice, his area of operations was confined to the railway line that ran along the Gudbrandsdal valley, which stretched from the Romsdal – where Aandalsnes was situated – to Lillehammer.

There were others who had their eyes on that stretch of line.

Chapter Fifteen

Three aircraft droned over the snow-covered Norwegian landscape. They were three-engined Junkers Ju 52 transports, flying in a tight "V" formation. Each carried 15 paratroops.

The dropping-zone had been well chosen. It was a snow-covered plateau on the northern side of the Gudbrandsdal, not far from a little village called Kvam. Here, the river Laagen, the road and the single-track railway that ran through the valley criss-crossed one another. The river, which turned in its course at this point to run east-west, was split here by an island about half a mile long. On either side the hills sloped sharply upward and were densely wooded with pines.

The drop, made from a height of 500 feet above ground level, was flawless. Within minutes all 45 paratroops were on the ground, unpacking the canisters that contained their mortars and machine-guns. The only injury was one slightly sprained ankle. As the men assembled for the descent into the valley, the transport aircraft flew off to the south, heading for Fornebu.

The commander of the paratroop detachment, Major Hahn, consulted his map. The village below the plateau consisted of a few low wooden buildings and could easily be turned into a strong defensive position. Entrenched there, Hahn and his men could block all movement along both road and railway. The English were reported to be landing in strength at Aandalsnes, and their first move would doubtless be to go to the aid of the Norwegians holding out at Lillehammer.

His orders were to stop them, and to hold Kvam until German reinforcements came up the road. There was something else, too. Somewhere between Kvam and the approaching German forces was a train which the German High Command was desperately anxious to capture, for whatever reason. Hahn could only speculate that it must contain high-ranking members of the Norwegian Government, perhaps even of the royal family, fleeing before the German advance. If the train appeared, Hahn was to stop it and ensure that it went no further.

Donning snowshoes – he had decided that skis would be an unnecessary encumbrance on this mission – Hahn issued his orders and led his men down through the trees. He told them to spread out and advance with caution, for he knew that Norwegian militia units were operating in the area. The men made little sound as they moved down the slope; dressed in their white winter-camouflage smocks they looked for all the world like phantoms. Little puffs of breath trailed behind them in the frosty air.

To Hahn's amazement, the village was deserted.

Removing their snowshoes, his men split up into small groups and checked out each house with an easy professionalism born of thorough training, and reported back with the news that they had found nothing. Even the fires were unlit, and the larders were empty of food.

He summoned his second in command, a young Austrian *Leutnant* named Maisel, and ordered him to take a patrol westwards for a mile or so along the railway line.

"And don't take any risks," he warned him. "We are not here to stick out our necks unnecessarily. If you run into trouble of any kind, or see anything at all out of place, get back here at once."

Maisel nodded and trotted off at the head of half a dozen men. He decided to follow the road that ran parallel with the railway line; it was higher up, and would afford a better view of what might lie ahead. Not a sound except their breathing and the crunch of their boots on the snow disturbed the silence.

After half a mile or so Maisel called a halt and checked his map against the features that were visible around him. It was a very good map, produced by the Norwegian Ordnance Survey Office, and it showed the most minute detail. What it did not show was a spur line, branching off the main track at this point and disappearing into the trees. The only feature revealed by the document here was a sawmill, nestling in the forest a few hundred yards to the right. Maisel reasoned that the spur line must be a recent feature, specially built to serve the mill. He made up his mind that it was worth investigating.

In single file, the patrol moved up the slope among the trees, keeping the spur line on the left. It was gloomy among the pines, and the shadows on the path ahead seemed to assume eerie shapes. Maisel felt a shiver run up his spine, then smiled to himself. This was, after all, the land of the trolls that had featured prominently in the fairytales of his childhood.

Suddenly, he stopped dead in his tracks, so abruptly that the next man in line almost collided with him. Maisel made an urgent signal and his men took cover, crouching down behind the pine trunks.

A light wind was blowing from the north, down the slope. It bore a smell with it, a smell which Maisel also associated with his childhood but couldn't quite place. It was an odour that mingled oil and ash and coal and smoke. All of a sudden he had it. It was the smell associated with railway engines, and the grime of stations.

He motioned to the others, wordlessly ordering them to stay where they were, and went on alone, creeping from tree to tree. After a while he halted again, peering ahead, trying to define what he was seeing. The line seemed to end in a tangle of pine branches, adding their freshly-cut resinous scent to the oily smell he had detected earlier.

Still keeping under cover of the trees, he stood up and went forward again, his sub-machine-gun at the ready, until he reached the barrier of branches. Stretching out a hand, he pulled at one and it came away to fall in the snow at his feet, bringing others down with it.

Maisel found himself staring at the rear end of a railway freight wagon.

There were others – a whole line of them, as he discovered on further investigation, coupled to an engine. He was about to climb up on to the footplate when a nearby shadow moved and an iron grip closed about his windpipe.

"What in the name of God are we going to do with them?" asked Captain Erling Jensen of nobody in particular, after the other six members of Maisel's patrol had been brought in. The Germans had been taken completely by surprise, overwhelmed before they could fire a shot by men who had risen from the very earth like the trolls of Maisel's childhood nightmares. Jensen was in command of the 30-strong party of Norwegian regular soldiers who had been assigned to guard the train and its precious cargo. Since leaving Lillehammer, their ranks had been augmented by militiamen who had been picked up here and there along the line, all of them anxious to join a unit that was making a stand against the enemy.

Jensen turned to Maisel, who like the other Germans was tied up securely. "How many more of you are there?" he rapped.

Maisel stared directly into the Norwegian's blue eyes. Strangely, he felt completely unafraid. He sensed instinctively that the Norwegians, men of a race that had been peace-loving for centuries, were not the kind to kill in cold blood.

"There are no more," he lied. "We are the only ones. And I demand that you release us immediately, or it will be the worse for you in the long run."

Concealed as they were in the forest, neither Jensen nor any of his men had witnessed the parachute drop, although he was sure that there had been one, as the Ju 52 transports had been seen passing overhead. The villagers of Kvam would certainly have seen it, had they been at home, but they had taken refuge in the buildings around the sawmill, where most of their menfolk worked, for fear that their hamlet might be bombed at any moment.

It was this same fear of air attack that had prompted Jensen to conceal the train in the forest. He knew little about air power; as far as he knew, the Germans were as proficient at bombing by night as they were by day, and he had seen and heard many German bombers passing overhead during the past 48 hours. His conclusion was that it would be better to stay put until the Allies arrived, as General Ruge had indicated they would.

He knew that he would obtain no information from the captured Germans, but he was convinced that they were part of a much larger force. To find out if his suspicions were correct, he despatched a couple of men in the direction of Kvam to see what was happening. Within minutes, they returned breathlessly with the news that more than 30 heavily-armed Germans were advancing along the road.

Carefully, for he was a methodical man, Jensen

weighed up the odds. With the addition of the 20 or so militiamen he had collected *en route* he had a force that was numerically superior to the enemy's, but his scouts reported that the Germans were carrying mortars and machine-guns, which he did not possess. He therefore issued orders for his men to deploy quickly into defensive positions in the woods between the concealed train and the main line. If the Germans made a move towards them they would be engaged; if they went past they would be left alone. It seemed the logical course of action to take.

In considering his options, however, Jensen had overlooked one particular simple fact. It was the trail of footprints left behind in the snow by Maisel's patrol.

In his own way, Major Hahn had been faced with a dilemma that was every bit as great as the Norwegian's. When Maisel had still not returned after an hour's absence, he had begun to feel the first twinges of worry. After another half-hour, he had decided to act. Convinced that some ill had befallen the seven-man patrol, he had decided to set out in search of it with the whole of his force except for two men, one of them the paratrooper nursing the sprained ankle, who had been left behind in the village with a machine-gun. And the trail of footprints, veering away into the forest, led him straight into trouble.

It was lucky that the first volley of Norwegian rifle fire only felled two of his men. The rest went to ground among the trees and began firing into the shadows – not haphazardly, for they were too well trained for that, but whenever they thought they detected a sign of movement. Pine branches, severed by bursts of gunfire, fell to the ground, showering the men beneath with snow.

Hahn realized that the Norwegians had planned their defensive positions skilfully. They commanded the higher ground and their flanks were well protected. Moreover, they appeared to be crack shots. He could use his mortars on them, but he had only a limited amount of mortar ammunition and he did not want to waste it. If British reinforcements came down the line, as he was certain they would, he would need every round.

He beckoned to his senior NCO, an experienced *Feldwebel* who had seen action in Poland and, before that, with the German *Kondor* Legion in the Spanish Civil War. The man, whose name was Baumer, crawled over and lay beside the officer, keeping his head well down.

"I'm going to divide my force," Hahn told him. "I want you to stay here with a dozen men and keep the Norwegians pinned down. I'll leave an MG with you. By the sound of things they only have rifles, so you should be able to beat them off easily if they try to attack you. I'm going back to the village with the rest. I've a feeling it won't be long before the Tommies turn up. I don't know if they will use the railway or motor transport, but either way you will be able to see them from here."

Baumer nodded. The road and adjacent railway

line were both visible through the cut in the trees that accommodated the spur line.

"When they do turn up," Hahn went on, "don't make a move until you hear my men in the village open fire. Then disengage here and make for the village through the trees. By the time you get there the Tommies will be in the process of deploying their forces. Attack them from the rear – try to cause as much confusion as possible. If you can't break through to join me, act on your own initiative. I'm sure you don't need me to tell you how to inflict the maximum possible damage, Baumer."

The NCO grinned. "All clear, sir," was all he said.

Quietly, Hahn and 20 or so of his men began to slip away from the scene, taking care to stay hidden from the Norwegians. They reached the road and began to make their way back towards Kvam. The sun had risen above the tops of the mountains now, casting the shadows of the men into sharp relief.

It was the shadows that Armstrong saw first, bobbing along the road ahead of him as he rounded a curve in the valley. He was flying at only 150 feet, with flaps lowered to reduce his speed, alert for any sign of movement. Suddenly, the shadows vanished as the men in the road threw themselves flat and became invisible.

Armstrong roared overhead, tilting a wing so that he could look down. There was no doubt about it; the bundles in the road were men, wearing white camouflage outfits.

He raised the flaps and opened the throttle, climbing and turning before descending into the valley from the opposite direction. As he flew past Kvam, a line of red dots rose towards him: tracer bullets. Whoever was in the village, they were unfriendly. Either that, or they didn't recognize a Spitfire. It was possible.

Then he saw the spur line. He had not noticed it earlier, having been distracted by the men in the road. He circled the spot, but could see nothing among the trees; but there was a clearing, with some buildings in it, and as he circled again he saw some people emerge from them, their upturned faces white as they gazed up at him. One or two of them waved, and he guessed that someone must have made out the RAF roundels under the Spitfire's wings.

Armstrong made another pass over the clearing, followed by a second run over the main railway line, but the white-smocked figures had disappeared. The trouble was that the Spitfire's high speed made it impossible to carry out an accurate visual reconnaissance in the few seconds available. Maybe Kalinski would learn more when he made a follow-up recce in the much slower Mureaux.

Armstrong climbed out of the valley again and set course for Lesjaskog, his mind working overtime. He knew that the missing train had passed various points on the line between Kvam and Lillehammer, because stationmasters along the route had confirmed it by telephone, but his reconnaissance of the line between Kvam and Aandalsnes had revealed no sign of it. Short of having driven itself into the river, it could only be concealed on the spur line he had just spotted; there was no other such line marked on his map of the route – a current Norwegian Army military map which was a couple of years more up to date than the one Hahn carried.

And if the men in the white smocks were Germans, and not Norwegians who had mistaken his Spitfire for a German aircraft, it might mean that the train had been captured.

He was still turning over the possibilities in his mind as he touched down on Lake Lesjaskog, noting as he taxied towards his dispersal that the thaw seemed to be setting in rapidly; even the packed snow piled on either side of the makeshift runway was beginning to melt. He turned the Spitfire tail-on to the clearing with a final burst of power and a shove on the rudder pedals, then switched off the engine and climbed from the cockpit, looking around for his ground crew, who were nowhere to be seen.

Kalinski, who as usual was fussing over the aircraft, provided an explanation.

"They didn't expect you back so soon," he said. "They have gone off for a sandwich. We can give you a hand to push the aircraft into the clearing, if you wish." He waved at his observer, a man with a completely unpronouncable name who spoke no English. He abandoned his task of feeding bullets into the ammunition belt that served the Mureaux' rear machine-gun and started to walk towards them.

Suddenly he stopped, his head cocked on one side, and shouted something in Polish. Kalinski answered him, then began to search the sky for the source of the faint droning they could all now hear. The visibility was good, with only a few streaks of high cirrus cloud – a sure sign that bad weather was on its way – to mar a pale blue sky. They saw the aircraft almost at once, silhouetted against the wispy cloud as they crawled high above the southern mountains. Armstrong counted 18 of them, flying in close formation, as though clinging to one another for security. They were close enough now for the men on the ground to see that they had twin engines. They were flying fairly high, at about 12,000 feet. After a few more moments, there was no longer any doubt as to their identity – even though at first Armstrong had thought that they looked like Blenheims.

"They're Junkers 88s!" he said urgently. "Come on – get under cover, fast!"

They dashed for the tree-line and threw themselves down, burrowing into the snow at the fringe of the pines. Armstrong looked up in time to see the leading Junkers break formation and enter a long dive, heading straight towards him, or so it seemed. The drone of its engines swelled to a howl.

In the cockpit of the leading bomber, the pilot centred his bomb-sight on the airstrip that ran part of the way across the frozen lake. The strip of cleared ice showed up dark grey against the surrounding snow, and had been easy to pick out from the height at which he had started his dive. With dive-brakes fully extended the Junkers screamed towards the ground at an angle of 60 degrees. The pilot found himself mentally ticking off the seconds; it took the Ju 88 around 20 seconds to dive from 13000 feet to its release height of 3200 ft. But all he had to do was hold the bomber steady and keep the target squarely in his sight; everything else was worked out for him automatically. The mental ticking-off of time was merely a habit.

He had counted 16 seconds when a harsh warning horn sounded. Four seconds later it ceased, and the pilot jabbed a button on the control column. The elevator tail-trimmer, which had been set for the dive, now returned to neutral and the Junkers began to pull itself out of the headlong rush towards the earth.

The button also activated the bomb release mechanism. A few seconds later, the four 1000 pound bombs carried on racks under the Junkers' wings dropped away automatically. The pull of gravity forced the bomber's four crew members down into their seats as the aircraft approached level flight, roaring across the lake. The pilot pulled it up into a steep climbing turn and looked back over his shoulder to see if his bombs had found their mark.

From the tenuous sanctuary of the pines, Armstrong, Kalinski and the latter's observer watched, hypnotized, as the four black projectiles hurtled towards the surface of the lake. An instant before the bombs impacted, the men clasped their hands over their ears and pushed their faces into the snow. The four bombs exploded in a single, shattering detonation, sending columns of water and great chunks of ice hurtling skywards. The air vibrated with the concussion, although the water damped down the effects of the shock wave before it reached the shore.

The air was filled with the scream of engines and more concussions as the other Ju 88s released their bombs in turn. Then, as suddenly as it had begun, the attack was over.

Armstrong and his companions sat up, their ears ringing, brushing snow from themselves. They stood up, rather groggily, and looked out over the lake. Kalinski looked at Armstrong, who was pale-faced.

"The first time you have been bombed?" he asked. Armstrong nodded.

"The first time is always the worst," the Pole told him. "My God, what a mess!"

He was referring to the lake. Where the airstrip had been, chunks of ice stood jaggedly on edge under an acrid smoke pall. Smoke was also rising from the trees at the edge of the lake some distance away, where the fighter squadron's Gladiators – those that were not out on patrol – were dispersed. Armstrong could see flames, and heard a crackle of exploding ammunition. Figures were running to and fro, trying ineffectually to extinguish the fires.

In the west, even at this distance, columns of smoke could be seen rising from Aandalsnes. Armstrong could see tiny dots that were aircraft twisting and turning in the sky between the lake and the town. A pencil-line of smoke appeared as if by magic, a dark streak against the blue. It grew and lengthened, probing down towards the earth, a series of bright flashes punctuating the smoke. An aircraft was plunging to its destruction, its fall marked by a holocaust of exploding fuel tanks. They watched it in fascination until Armstrong broke the spell.

"The Spitfire! Come on – let's get her under cover!"

Armstrong's aircraft was still intact, and so, for the time being, was the patch of ice on which it stood. They ran towards it, Kalinski's observer in the lead.

The next instant Armstrong was flat on his face on the ice, the wind thumped out of him as Kalinski brought him down with a tackle. There was a confused sensation of cannon fire mixed with a thunderous noise of engines, a series of rapid explosions, and a scream that was abruptly cut off. Dazedly, not comprehending what had happened, Armstrong raised his head.

A few yards away the Spitfire lay collapsed and crumpled on one wing, shattered by cannon shells. Nearby, the Polish observer lay spreadeagled on his back, a pool of blood already spreading and freezing around his body.

The Messerschmitt 110, which must have formed part of the Junkers' fighter escort and which no-one had seen, was already climbing away into the southern sky.

Chapter Sixteen

Armstrong and Kalinski climbed down from the Mureaux and looked around. Four Gladiators had also landed at the muddy airstrip just outside Aandalsnes; they had been engaged in the air battle to the east of the town and had escaped the destruction of the frozen lake base. The Poles assigned to the defence of Lesjaskog were also making for Aandalsnes by road, together with the RAF ground crews.

Armstrong still shuddered as he recalled the hair-raising take-off from Lesjaskog, the ice breaking up under the wheels of Kalinski's aircraft even as it lurched into the air with seconds to spare. He was full of admiration for the Pole, who certainly knew what he was about. The two of them now trudged along the road that led into the town, ankle-deep in slush, and sought out Brigade Headquarters.

The German air attack had inflicted substantial damage on the little harbour; the smoke they had seen earlier came from a freighter offshore, which was well ablaze and listing. Work parties were busily clearing paths through the wreckage so that the flow of supplies to the troops onshore might continue. The streets were congested with transport, much of it comprising requisitioned Norwegian lorries.

The two pilots eventually located Brigade HQ in a school. It was crammed with personnel, and the newcomers hovered uncertainly for a minute or two until they spotted Colonel Gough, in earnest conversation with a Norwegian officer. They pushed their way through the throng and waited until the Army officer noticed them. The anxiety on his face was obvious.

"I'm glad you got away all right," he said. "What about your aircraft?"

"The Spitfire's a write-off," Armstrong told him, "but the Mureaux is in one piece. Captain Kalinski's observer was killed in the attack, so I hitched a lift with him. We got off by the skin of our teeth. The aircraft is out at the strip."

"Did you see anything on your recce?" Gough asked. "We are desperate for information about what's happening between here and Lillehammer."

"I went as far as Kvam," Armstrong told him. "It looks as though the village is in enemy hands. At any rate, I was fired on. My guess is that they've dropped some paratroops. I saw some on the road, and they seemed to be wearing white camouflage overalls."

He fished in the pocket of his fleece-lined flying jacket and pulled out the crumpled map. "There's a spur line just here," he said, his finger indicating the spot. "It disappears into the trees, and if you look closely you'll see a cluster of buildings in this clearing. There were people there, too, and some of them waved. Pulling all the threads together, it's my guess that our missing train is hidden somewhere up that line."

"Did you see anything – anything at all – to indicate whether the train might have been captured?"

The pilot shook his head. "No. But then, I'm not even sure that it's there at all. I'm just going on guesswork. I'd hoped that Captain Kalinski might have been able to find out more. The Spitfire's speed doesn't give one time to make much of an assessment."

Gough nodded, and spent a few moments deep in thought, his chin resting on his hand. Then his head came up and he looked at each man in turn. His earlier look of anxiety, Armstrong noted, had been replaced by one of firm decision.

"Right. We've wasted enough time here. Nip into that room there— " he pointed to a door that stood ajar " —and give me a minute to contact the Brigade Commander. Then we'll hold a council of war."

Armstrong and Kalinski went through into the small room, and saw at once that it must be the head teacher's office. There were bookshelves around the walls, and a globe stood on a pedestal in one corner. The centrepiece was a large desk.

"I wonder where they keep the cane?" Armstrong muttered. Kalinksi looked at him, puzzled, and then smiled in understanding. "In Poland we use the birch," he said. Maybe in Norway the children are all well-behaved."

After a few minutes Colonel Gough entered the room, followed by two British Army officers: he introduced them as Major Stavely of the Green

Howards and Captain Bush of the King's Own Yorkshire Light Infantry.

"Very well," Gough said, once the brief formalities had been completed, "here's the picture. Where's that map of yours, Armstrong? It's the only decently detailed one we've got."

Armstrong unfolded the map and smoothed it out on the desktop. Gough tapped his finger on the Gudbrandsdal, frowning, and moved it on to Lillehammer.

"By now, 148 Brigade should have been well on its way to relieve the Norwegians here," he said, "but it isn't. The main problem is a shortage of transport, both road and rail, and of course the confusion created by the air raid hasn't helped. Now, 148 Brigade is assembling and will advance on Dombaas as soon as sufficient transport is available, but from the information supplied by Flight Lieutenant Armstrong the Germans may be on the way to beating us to it. The Norwegians are still holding on at Lillehammer, but by all accounts they've about had it, and may well cave in before 148 Brigade gets through to them."

His finger retraced the course of the railway line from Dombaas to its terminus at Aandalsnes.

"The only troops we have in position so far along the line," he continued, "are the Royal Marines, bless 'em, who are holding key points between Verma and Lesja, this side of Dombaas. Their function is not offensive; it is to defend the approaches to Aandalsnes along the Gudbrandsdal. There is also a single Norwegian battalion a few miles to the south, which is being slowly reinforced by militia, or so I am led to believe."

He gazed at the two Army officers. "That's it, in essence. Now, what I want you to do is to take two companies by road through to Kvam as a spearhead force for 148 Brigade. I have cleared this with the Brigade Commander. Upon reaching Kvam, your first task will be to eliminate any enemy troops you may find there, and to secure a train which we believe may be concealed in the woods, just here. Once you have dealt with the Germans, your only priority will be to ensure that this train remains in our hands. When you are relieved by the rest of 148 Brigade – and I hope that this will only take a matter of hours – you will escort the train back here, to Aandalsnes."

The two officers looked at one another in perplexity. Armstrong smiled inwardly, certain that they were going to ask the same question he had put to Gough soon after his arrival at Lesjaskog. He was right, but he was wrong in his assumption about what Gough's answer would be.

"Well," the Colonel said, "I don't suppose it can do any harm to put you fully in the picture. After all, the Germans would appear to know what the train contains. But mind you – not a word to anyone else outside this room."

Briefly, Gough told them the story of the train's cargo. When he had finished, they looked at him in utter silence. Major Stavely was the first to break it. He cleared his throat. "Did you say fifty-five *million* dollars, sir?"

Gough nodded. "That is correct, Major. About eleven million pounds Sterling, but worth far more to the Nazi war effort if they get their hands on it."

"Good Lord! I could buy Yorkshire with that," Bush exclaimed. Gough smiled thinly. "No doubt, Captain. A fair slice of it, at least. So now you will appreciate how important it is for us to get that gold out of the country. We have to assume the worse case – that Norwegian resistance will collapse because we simply can't provide enough assistance, and that the country will be quickly overrun. I hope it won't come to that, but we can't afford to take chances. There's a fast cruiser standing by offshore to take the gold on board, and has been for the past couple of days. I can tell you that her skipper is far from happy; the Germans have had a go at bombing him twice already. That's all – except for one thing. I am assigning Captain Kalinski and his aircraft to you for observation duties. Make the most of him – his is the only observation aircraft we have left."

Kalinski stepped forward and clicked his heels, a difficult exercise in flying boots. "There is just one thing, Colonel," he said. "I no longer have an observer. He was killed in the attack on the lake."

"I'm sorry," Gough said with sincerity. "We shall have to find you a replacement for him."

"There's no need, sir," Armstrong interjected. "I'll fly with the Captain. After all, I haven't got an aircraft of my own any more."

"Thank you, Flight Lieutenant. I'm grateful to you. It remains only for me to wish you the very best of luck. Report back to me as soon as you can. I fear we may not have much time."

They saluted and left the room. Gough sighed heavily and sat down at the big desk, letting his thoughts run on for a while, trying to put events so far into perspective. It had been no easy task to land the Allied forces at Aandalsnes, nor for that matter at Namsos on the other side of Trondheim. Despite the fact that many of their officers were inexperienced, the troops had responded magnificently to their task; not only had they got ashore, but they had succeeded in obliterating all traces of their landing in record time, even though they had the benefit of only about three hours of darkness. Consequently, there had been a period of respite before the German reconnaissance aircraft discovered what was going on, and called in the bombers.

But the troops lacked all the essentials of equipment with which to fight a winter war. They had no skis, and even if these had been available the troops were not trained to use them. Some French *Chasseurs Alpins* who had been put ashore at Namsos were equipped with skis, and would have been invaluable – except that some quartermaster had neglected to pack the straps with which to attach the skis to their feet, without which they were completely useless. They normally used mules for transport in the mountains, but these had not turned up in Norway either.

The British troops had been issued with fur coats, special boots and socks to ward off the cold. The only problem was that the kit was so cumbersome that it was quite impossible to fight in it. As one of Gough's fellow officers put it, the men looked like paralyzed bears.

As for the deployment of tanks, heavy artillery and supporting aircraft, thought Gough, there was no problem at all, because there were none.

The RAF's fighter force, pitifully small to start with, was now reduced to two or three machines that had survived the attack on the frozen lake, and even they were starved of fuel.

Deep down, Gough knew that the Allied expedition to Norway was not going to succeed. It had never had any hope of succeeding. But it had to try.

At the other end of the Gudbrandsdal, similar thoughts were passing through the mind of General Ruge, the Norwegian commander. The situation of his forces was becoming increasingly desperate. Four columns of German troops, equipped with tanks and artillery and constantly supported from the air, were pushing rapidly north, constantly outflanking the gallant but inexperienced Norwegian forces that tried to block their path.

Already – it was now 18 April – the enemy had advanced along the Glomma valley and taken Elverum, near the Swedish border. A second column captured Hamar, midway along the eastern shore of Lake Mjosa, on the same day. Across the lake, below Gjorvik, the enemy were advancing on Raufoss, bent on capturing the only munitions factory that still remained in Norwegian hands.

To the west, the Germans were making a rapid

advance along the east bank of the Randsfjord, putting them in a position from which they could outflank the whole of Ruge's defences around Mjosa. With the last of his reserves committed and his men exhausted, rapid reinforcement by the Allies was the general's only remaining hope.

So it was that, when a messenger arrived from the telephone exchange with the news that an Allied force had left Aandalsnes and was heading into the Gudbrandsdal, Ruge's spirits soared.

"At last!" he exclaimed. "How many troops?"

The messenger hesitated before replying. "I fear – less than two hundred, General," he said lamely, knowing what the effect would be.

General Ruge slumped in a chair and buried his face in his hands. Up to a moment ago, his heart had been filled with hopelessness. Now there was nothing but bitterness.

The two companies of troops reached Dombaas as Norway's brief night was falling to find the town in ruins. Norwegian troops, civilians and some Royal Marines were moving among the smouldering wreckage of once-neat homes. The British soldiers were aghast at the devastation, and willingly set about helping wherever and however they could. Major Stavely, their commander, noticed that the townspeople virtually ignored the new arrivals, and wondered why. Then he realised that the answer was simple. They were in a state of shock, still unable to comprehend the disaster that had overwhelmed their peaceful existence.

"Air attack," explained a Royal Marines lieutenant simply. "We were at Lesja, a few miles up the road, and we saw them going in. Funny thing," he added, waving a hand at the destruction, "the Jerries missed both the road and the railway line. You'd almost think it was intentional."

"It would be," Stavely told him. "They'll need to keep both intact if they're planning on driving towards the coast, which no doubt they are."

He glanced at his watch. His column had made good progress, so he decided to remain at Dombaas for an hour or so to let his men go on helping with cleaning the place up. Besides, he thought, they could do with a brew. After that they would press on towards Kvam, which was still some 30 miles distant, and halt at a place called Kjorem, which according to the map was about five miles short of the main objective. He would then advance on Kvam at first light, for he had no wish to go blundering into trouble in the dark.

At Kvam, Major Hahn was also anticipating first light, but for a different reason. His signaller had finally managed to establish contact with advance units of the German forces on the offensive in the Lillehammer area, and he had been advised that a second airdrop would take place in the morning, this time to the south of the valley. With this reinforcement, he would not only be able to take his principal objective – the train, around which the Norwegians were still keeping his men pinned down – but also form a much stronger blocking position than he had at first anticipated. In his mind's eye, he could already see the Führer hanging the *Ritterkreuz* – perhaps even a higher decoration – around his neck.

A few miles to the west, the Allied convoy was moving steadily along the tortuous road through the Norwegian night that was not really night at all, for there was no darkness such as the men were used to in more southerly climes. But it was enough to shelter them from the prying eyes of German reconnaissance aircraft, and Major Stavely was convinced that with luck, his small force would achieve the desired element of surprise.

The trucks reached Kjorem before daybreak and Stavely ordered the Norwegian drivers to pull the vehicles off the road into the shelter of the trees. Concealing the vehicles did not present a problem, for the woods were dense. He also ordered the troops to strip off their cumbersome winter clothing and stow it on the trucks. The men would fight the coming battle in light webbing: belt, braces and ammunition pouches. Stavely was concerned that his troops were very lightly armed; apart from rifles and Brens, they had only two 3-inch mortars and a solitary 25-mm Hotchkiss anti-tank gun. It would have to do.

Leaving the trucks in charge of their uncomplaining Norwegian drivers, Stavely led his men towards Kvam, filtering through the woods in small groups under a gradually lightening sky. It was heavy going, for the snow was deep in places between the pines, and despite the cold the troops were soon sweating, grateful that they were no longer burdened by heavy clothing. It took them three hours, with several halts on the way, before Stavely's map told him that they were within three-quarters of a mile of Kvam. Ordering another halt, he crept forward with an NCO, Sergeant Neesham, to ascertain what might lie ahead.

They had gone barely 100 yards when a machine-gun chattered, frighteningly close. Both men threw themselves flat in the snow and lay there, breathing hard, before daring to raise their heads slightly.

It was a trail of smoke, drifting through the trees, that drew their attention to the weapon's position. It fired again, loosing off two short bursts at some unseen target up the slope. A crackle of rifle shots answered it, and a ricochet whined away between the tree-trunks.

Stavely had left orders with Captain Bush to bring up the rest of the men if there was any hint of trouble, and was about to send Neesham back to make sure that they advanced cautiously, without being seen, when he saw Bush himself crouching behind a tree only a few yards back. Seeing that his superior officer had spotted him, Bush kitten-crawled through the snow until he lay alongside. Panting with the effort, he whispered: "There's a Norwegian officer back there with us, sir. His scouts have been shadowing us for ages; wanted to make certain whose side we were on. The train's here all right, up there in the woods, and he's in charge of it. Those are Jerry paratroops up ahead; he says his men have captured a few. There are others in Kvam village."

"Does he know how many machine-guns?" Stavely whispered back.

"Just one here, sir, but others in the village. Mortars, too."

"Right. Let's deal with this lot first. Are the men coming up?"

"Already moving into position, sir."

"Good. I want two Brens up here right away. We'll get that MG out of the way first. Nip back to our Norwegian chum, and tell him to go back to his train. When he hears the grenade go off, I want his chaps to open up with everything they've got. Five minutes from now, OK?" Bush nodded, consulting his watch, and slipped away.

The two Bren gunners arrived – making enough noise to wake the dead, in Stavely's opinion, although there was no sign that their approach had been detected by the enemy – and he urgently motioned them under cover. They lay prone, their weapons cocked and ready, sighting on targets they could not see as yet.

Stavely concentrated on his wrist-watch, seeing the second hand move around the face with painful slowness. At last, it reached the vertical.

"Now, Sergeant," the officer said quietly.

Neesham had been clutching a Mills bomb for some time, ready primed with its pin removed. An expert grenade thrower, he half rose and hurled the bomb at the spot where he had pinpointed the enemy machine-gun. There was a flash and a puff of smoke, followed instantly by the crack of the explosion and an almost simultaneous screaming that jarred Stavely's nerves. He had never heard a noise like it, a raw mixture of pain, shock, disbelief and naked terror.

"Fire!" he roared at the top of his voice.

From positions up the slope, where the train was concealed, and from the flank, bullets raked the Germans where they lay in shallow foxholes among the trees. Beside Stavely, the two Brens stuttered, chopping at the enemy in short bursts. For a while the Germans returned the fire, but then, realizing that their position was no longer tenable, Baumer, their NCO, gave the order to withdraw. White-clothed figures leaped to their feet and flitted away through the trees, making for the village. The bullets sought some of them out and they fell headlong, but the majority got away.

"Well," Stavely said to Bush a few minutes later, as the Norwegians set about the grim task of collecting the dead and wounded Germans, "now they know we're here. Let's hope we can flush the rest out before their pals come up the road. And for God's sake, somebody tell the Norwegians to get this damned train ready to move."

Chapter Seventeen

The valley reverberated to the rattle of gunfire and the explosions of mortar bombs. Aided by the Norwegians, Major Stavely had deployed his men as expertly as possible around Kvam, completely surrounding the village, and had also positioned platoons on either bank of the River Laagen and on the island that divided it, on guard for enemy forces approaching from the east.

He had quickly come to realize that whoever commanded the German paratroops was no novice, which of course Major Hahn was not. The German had not wasted time; he had turned the village into a formidable strongpoint, setting his men to felling trees in order to provide the houses with extra protection and to construct solid mortar pits. His machine-guns commanded a wide field of fire, covering every angle of approach.

The one thing that worried Major Hahn was that he might run out of ammunition before help arrived. Luckily, the English and their Norwegian friends had not been foolhardy enough to try an assault over open ground; they would have been cut to shreds, of course, but his men would have expended valuable ammunition in the process. As it was, the Allied commander seemed content to keep him pinned down, lobbing the occasional mortar bomb into his position.

In fact, Major Stavely was far from content. Recognizing that any assault on the enemy positions would lead to unacceptable casualties, he was waiting anxiously for the wind to change. If he couldn't take the village by a head-on assault, the next best bet was to smoke out the Germans, or at least generate enough smoke for his men to attack under its cover.

The wind was gradually moving round to the west. Just another few degrees, and he would give orders for the group of men stationed among the trees with petrol-filled cans to set fire to the woods. Although no woodsman, he knew enough about pines to be certain that they would burn.

Stavely had set up his HQ in a house nestling on the hillside several hundred yards from the village; it was not an exposed position, but he had a good view of the houses below and the river beyond. Its rightful occupants, a young couple with two children who had been with those who had taken refuge at the sawmill, had wanted to return, but he had regretfully turned them away, insisting that it would be too dangerous. He had been right, of course, but their obvious disappointment had been hard to bear.

"Sir." It was Sergeant Neesham, who had been on observation duty outside.

"Yes, Sergeant, what is it?"

"Aircraft, sir. Comin' up the valley. Don't think it's a Jerry, sir."

Stavely went outside and looked up through a gap in the trees. A moment later he saw it, flying at a safe height outside the range of small-arms fire. It waggled its wings, circled the area and then flew off to the south. Stavely smiled.

"That's our observation aircraft, sergeant," he told the NCO. "Gone to see what's over the hill, no doubt."

Stavely knew exactly what was over the hill 20 minutes later, and he was wishing that he didn't. The aircraft returned, dipped low over the valley before heading south again, and a breathless runner came floundering through the snow, carrying the message container it had dropped. The major pulled off the lid and extracted the roll of paper that was inside, reading the message that was hand-printed on it with growing alarm:

> THREE TANKS AND APPROX 50 INFANTRY APPROACHING FROM SOUTH, FIVE MILES. ALSO TOWED ARTILLERY AND TRUCKS. WILL INVESTIGATE FURTHER.

"That's all we need," Stavely said, as he informed his officer of the new development. "How the hell did they get this far? What's happened to the Norwegians south of the river?"

In the freezing tandem cockpit of the Mureaux, Armstrong and Kalinski were asking themselves much the same question. The enemy force was advancing through the mountains along a road which, according to his map, should not have been there at all. But it was there all right, threading its way through the peaks for 30 miles, and Armstrong could only assume that it had been spotted by the ever-present German reconnaissance aircraft.

He frowned. Somewhere around here, according to Colonel Gough, there ought to be a Norwegian Army battalion, but there was no sign of it. If it was not in a position to halt or at least slow down the enemy column, then the troops at Kvam would soon be in serious trouble.

There was no intercom in the Mureaux apart from a primitive speaking-tube; it was easier, and more effective, for pilot and observer to shout at one another. In any case, Armstrong had no trouble in understanding his pilot's signals. With a sweep of the arm, Kalinski indicated that he was going down to attack the approaching enemy.

"Oh, God," Armstrong muttered to himself. "This is unreal. Any second now and I'll wake up."

But it was real, and despite himself he laughed out loud, recalling the words of a pilot he'd met who had flown Hawker Audax biplanes against dissident tribesmen in Iraq before the war. "Piece of cake, old boy," the veteran had told him. "You just creep up on 'em, gun the engine a few times to frighten the horses, then give 'em a good thrashing with the old Lewis gun!"

Armstrong had a feeling that the Mureaux would probably have acquitted itself quite well in Iraq. But the enemy down there ahead of it now were not poorly-armed Iraqis on horseback, but well-armed Germans with tanks and machine-guns, and the immediate future appeared anything but rosy. Anyhow, he thought resignedly as Kalinski pushed down the aircraft's nose, he didn't have much choice in the matter.

He had already checked his MAC machine-gun, and now he cocked it and swivelled it round on its mounting so that it was pointing downwards over the side of the cockpit. He had no forward field of view, but he would know when they were at the target when Kalinski's gun opened up. The Mureaux vibrated as the speed built up, the slipstream howling past the struts like a flock of demons in full flight.

The aircraft shuddered as the pilot opened fire, then levelled out of its headlong dive, forcing Armstrong towards the floor of the cockpit and momentarily throwing him off balance. Recovering, he grabbed his gun again and peered over the side, just in time to see a convoy of trucks, nose to tail. He raked them with the gun as the aircraft shot past, although with scant hope that he had actually hit anything.

Somebody was firing back, though, because there was a sharp toc-toc-toc and three neat holes appeared in the aircraft's left wing, close to where one of the struts joined it and too close to Armstrong's head for comfort. Then, suddenly, he was being thrown all over the rear cockpit again as Kalinski stood the aircraft on its tail. He heard the pilot shouting a string of words, and even though they were incomprehensible to him, being in Polish, he was convinced that they were not of a polite nature.

Armstrong had a dazed impression, no more than

a fleeting glimpse, of huge dark shapes all around him. Then the Mureaux turned violently upside down as a massive slipstream caught it, buffeting it out of control. The snow-covered earth and the mountain peaks whirled crazily around him and he closed his eyes, certain that they were going to crash but feeling strangely calm and detached about it all; then, miraculously, Kalinski had the groaning and protesting Mureaux under control again, returning it to the state of level flight to which it was more accustomed.

Kalinski steep-turned the aircraft so that its nose was pointing north, towards the River Laagen. He was yelling at the top of his voice, giving vent to what sounded like wild Red Indian war whoops, and gesticulating ahead. Armstrong tried to see around him, peering between the struts and the engine cowling past the whirling propeller blades. The he saw what was making the pilot so excited, and could hardly believe his own eyes.

Dead ahead of the Mureaux was a formation of six Junkers 52 transports. There was no mistaking them. And as he watched, sticks of parachutists began to tumble from their exit doors, their parachute canopies blossoming as they drifted down towards a relatively flat snow-covered expanse below, a place where the valley walls diverged.

Armstrong realized that they must have flown slap through the middle of the Junkers formation, which was now turning away, its task completed. For a moment he thought that Kalinski was going in pursuit of the lumbering transports, but the Pole had other ideas. Lumbering or not, the Ju 52s were only marginally slower than the Mureaux, and overhauling them would be a practical impossibility. There were easier targets.

Yelling "Shoot!" to Armstrong, Kalinski swept down on the descending paratroops, his gun chattering. The men had dropped as usual from a low altitude and were in the act of landing, hastily trying to disentangle themselves from their parachute harnesses. As the aircraft roared past them, a few feet above the ground, Armstrong hosed bullets at them from his rear gun. It was only when he saw men collapsing, their white smocks spattered with red blotches, that he realized he was killing them.

But some were firing back, intent on killing *him*. There was a sudden loud thump and the Mureaux lurched. Alarmed, heart in mouth, Armstrong looked over the side of the cockpit and then drew back, coughing, as grey fuel vapour swirled around him.

"They've hit the tank," he heard Kalinski shout. "Got to get her down before she catches fire. I'll get as close to the river as I can."

Fire, Armstrong thought, clutching the side of the cockpit in terror. Please God, not that. Get her down *now*, you crazy Polish bastard!

But Kalinski flew on, the aircraft descending steadily, heading along the mountain pass towards where the road began its tortuous descent through the pines to the river below. The stench of petrol was almost unbearable. At last, when he had put a couple of miles between himself and the enemy paratroops, Kalinski decided that it was time to set the Mureaux down.

In response to a shouted command from the pilot, Armstrong tightened his seat harness and hung on for dear life, watching with a kind of paralysis as the mountain slopes rushed past the aircraft's wing-tips. With flaps fully extended, the pilot found a straight bit of road and slammed the Mureaux down on its sturdy undercarriage. There was a fearsome crash and the aircraft bounced into the air again. The next instant, Armstrong was slammed brutally against the front of the cockpit as the undercarriage came into contact with soft snow and the aircraft decelerated from 50 miles per hour to zero in a couple of seconds.

He found himself staring at the sky as the tail rose vertically, and had the presence of mind to duck down into the cockpit as the machine turned over on its back. The broad parasol wing acted as a cushion, the struts cracking and splintering as its upper surface struck the snow-covered road.

Hanging upside down, his head only a matter of inches from the road, bruised and dazed, Armstrong loosened his straps and stretched out an arm, bracing his hand firmly against the ground. Then he unfastened the harness completely and quickly extended his other arm, letting his limbs take the weight as he lowered himself from the cockpit and crawled out from underneath the shattered wing.

Smoke was trickling from beneath the aircraft's engine cowling. Kalinski was still in the front cockpit, his arms dangling and waving feebly.

He was half-conscious and muttering something unintelligible. Armstrong tried to support him with one arm as he fumbled inside the cockpit, seeking the pilot's harness release. It seemed to be locked tight. Armstrong felt panic beginning to hamper his movements; the smoke was becoming thicker.

Suddenly, there was someone beside him. A knife blade flashed, biting into the harness. Strong arms caught the pilot as, freed at last, he dropped head first from his seat. Then, still dazed and only half aware of what he was doing, Armstrong was helping to drag Kalinski clear of the wreck into the shelter of some boulders.

A second or two later, the Mureaux' fuel tank ignited with a dull thud, sending a column of thick black smoke rolling up into the sky.

Shaking his head to clear it, Armstrong looked at the man who had come so unexpectedly to the rescue. Like the German paratroops, he wore a white smock, and for a moment alarm surged through the Englishman. Then, with a rush of relief, he realized that the man was a Norwegian soldier. He also saw that there were more of them on the mountain slopes; they had raised their heads from their defensive positions to see what was happening.

"Do you speak English?" he enquired. The Norwegian grinned at him. "Sure," he replied. "Five years in British Merchant Navy. Can swear like bloody trooper."

"Listen," Armstrong said urgently. "There's a force of German paratroops a couple of miles back. You must have seen them drop. But just behind them there's a column of tanks, artillery and infantry. We counted three tanks up front, and half a dozen guns. Don't know how many troops, maybe a couple of hundred."

"Sure," said the former merchant seaman. "We watch them. Make little surprise for the shitty bastards here. You go now quick, before fuckers arrive. River three kilometres that way. Go straight down hill, and you come out near Kvam. Your troops there." A sudden shrill whistle attracted his attention, and he looked up at the hillside, where a soldier was waving his arms. He bent over Kalinski, who was now sitting up, and seized him by the armpits, pulling him to his feet. He draped one of the Pole's arms over Armstrong's shoulder and gave him a friendly push.

"Go now quick. Get into trees. Soon we fight."

Armstrong nodded his thanks and shook the Norwegian's hand before turning and plodding off in the direction the man had indicated. After a few tottering steps, Kalinski came fully to his senses and removed his arm from his companion's shoulders.

"I can manage now, thanks," he said. "Just felt a little shaky, that's all." He managed a weak grin. "Now neither of us has an aeroplane," he added.

They reached the shelter of the trees and started off down the long slope towards the river, stumbling through the snow. Behind them, the Norwegian ex-sailor picked up his rifle, resumed his former position and waited.

The German paratroops advanced in two files, one on either side of the narrow road, cautiously approaching the spot where Kalinski's aircraft still burned furiously. Just before they reached it, the Norwegians opened fire, killing and wounding several. Dragging their wounded with them the Germans withdrew, one group expertly covering another as it pulled back, the whole force retreating several hundred yards.

Soon afterwards, the first German shells began bursting on the hillsides.

Chapter Eighteen

As they stumbled down the slope, Armstrong and Kalinski found that the mountain road ceased to exist, becoming little more than a track winding between the trees, but one still wide enough to allow the passage of the Mk III *Panzers* and the artillery the Germans were bringing up.

Behind them, the two men heard the boom of explosions as the enemy guns opened up on the Norwegian positions. There was firing ahead of them, too, in the valley, and something else: smoke. They could smell it long before they saw its tendrils drifting through the trees, and it carried the strong scent of burning conifers.

Suddenly, Kalinski gave a hiss and seized his companion by the arm, pulling him down on to his knees at the base of a tree. White-clad figures were flitting through the trees farther down the slope, pausing briefly to take snapshots at unseen targets before continuing their flight.

"What do you make of it?" Kalinski whispered in Armstrong's ear.

"At a guess, I'd say our chaps have driven the Germans out of the village," Armstrong whispered back. Until now, he had had no idea where the track joined the valley floor in relation to Kvam, but the direction in which the Germans were heading told him that the village must be somewhere off to the left.

"Come on," Armstrong said urgently, "we've got to get back and let the troops know exactly what's heading their way. Listen to that!" He gave a jerk of his head, indicating the way they had come. The explosions of artillery shells had given way to rifle and machine-gun fire, which meant that the enemy must be assaulting the dug-in Norwegians.

"They haven't a hope of holding on," he said grimly. "Let's get going."

Checking first to make sure that there were no more Germans in the vicinity, the two airmen doubled away through the trees, keeping low and stopping every so often to watch and listen for signs of trouble. They had gone just over a mile, by Armstrong's calculation, when several shots rang out. Splinters of wood whirled from a tree trunk a few feet above Armstrong's head and he threw himself flat, followed a split second later by Kalinski.

Armstrong was in no doubt about who was doing the shooting; there was no mistaking the dull report of a Lee-Enfield .303 rifle.

"Hold your fire!" he yelled at the top of his voice. "We're British!" It was only half-true, but that didn't matter under the prevailing circumstances.

There was a pause lasting a few seconds, then a voice with a trace of a Yorkshire accent shouted back, "All right, come forward slowly. But keep your hands in the air!"

They advanced cautiously, emerging from the trees opposite the eastern end of the island that divided the River Laagen. An arm rose out of a foxhole, waving them on. A few seconds later, they stumbled breathlessly into positions on the south bank of the river that were occupied by soldiers of the Nineteenth Regiment of Foot: Alexandra, Princess of Wales's Own Yorkshire Regiment, more popularly known as the Green Howards.

A young subaltern rose from his foxhole and regarded the two newcomers dubiously. A Smith and Wesson .38 revolver dangled from his hand.

"Who the blazes are you two?" he demanded to know.

"Flight Lieutenant Armstrong, and this is Captain Kalinski. We were shot down."

The young officer's face brightened. "Oh, I know who you are. I say, bad luck, though. About being shot down, I mean." He gave the men a cigarette apiece; Kalinski shook his head but Armstrong accepted one gratefully, his pipe being at Aandalsnes with the rest of his belongings – which, fortunately, his ground crew had managed to rescue for him before they began the trek back from Lesjaskog.

The valley floor was clogged with dense smoke from the pines that were burning on the other side of the river. The officer confirmed what Armstrong had suspected; that the trees had been deliberately set on fire to cover an assault on the village.

"Listen," the pilot said, "I've got to see Major Stavely urgently." In a few sentences, he explained the size and composition of the enemy force that would shortly be descending through the woods.

"We wondered what the firing was," the subaltern said thoughtfully. "It looks as though the Norwegians are catching a packet, then."

Armstrong nodded. "They can't possibly hold on." Already, he noticed that the distant firing had died away to the odd desultory shot. "Keep your eyes open for the survivors, if there are any. They are wearing white smocks, like the Jerry paratroopers, so it will be easy to mistake them for the enemy if they filter down through the woods."

"Thanks. We will." The Green Howard officer summoned a corporal and instructed him to take the two pilots to Major Stavely's HQ. The river was still frozen over, and so presented no obstacle. Armstrong and Kalinski shook the subaltern's hand and wished him good luck, with the certainty that he was going to need it.

On the opposite slope the fire was beginning to die down as the wind, continuing to veer towards the north, shifted the path of the flames towards the open ground bordering the river bank. The smoke had served its purpose and the village had been taken with remarkably few casualties; in fact, Stavely wondered why the Germans had departed with such alacrity. He had expected them to put up stiffer resistance.

"So that's it," he said, as the story told by the two pilots confirmed their earlier sighting of the approaching enemy force. "With reinforcements as close as that, they had no need to hold on to the village any more and risk further casualties. And, with tanks and artillery, the Huns can afford to bide their time; they can simply stand off and shell us out of our positions, and their isn't a damned thing we can do about it." His tone was understandably bitter.

He turned to Captain Bush, who was in attendance. "Johnny, off you go and find Captain Jensen. Tell him to get that bloody train on the move, as fast as he can. If it's still here in half an hour it will probably be blown off the track." Bush nodded and left hurriedly. As an afterthought, he said to Armstrong, "You and Captain Kalinski had better go along with the train. There's really nothing more you can do here. If you happen to bump into the rest of 148 Brigade, for God's sake tell them to get a move on."

Armstrong knew that Stavely was right. The two airmen would be a hindrance rather than a help if they stayed. They bade farewell to the major and hurried off in the footsteps of his second in command.

Only minutes after the departure of the train – an event viewed with much relief by Major Stavely – the Norwegian survivors of the action to the south of the valley began to filter back through the British positions. Exhausted and depleted though they were, they at once offered to join in the defence of Kvam. Stavely refused, recognizing that they had fought to the brink of their endurance, and ordered them back to the sawmill in the woodland clearing, with instructions that they were to be given hot food and time to rest. The weary men had scarcely cleared the area of the village when a German tank was sighted, nosing its way out of the woods about 2000 yards ahead of the forward defensive positions.

From his observation post, Stavely could clearly see the enemy through the thinning smoke, which tended to cling to the valley floor. For that reason, he was worried in case the smoke might interfere with the field of fire of his outposts; however, it would hamper the enemy equally, if not more.

Two more tanks emerged from the woods, followed by some artillery which was immediately wheeled into position on the river bank. Through his binoculars, Stavely could see groups of infantry, some in white smocks and others in standard issue field grey German uniforms, also moving into position under the concealment of the trees. Some scurried across the frozen surface of the river and went to ground beside the railway line. Of the trucks that had brought the infantry there was no sign; they would, he guessed, be held well back, just as his own were.

Stavely swore under his breath. If he had possessed just one battery of 25-pounder field guns he could have blown the whole lot to kingdom come. As it was, he would have to sit tight and take whatever the enemy threw at him, waiting until their troops came within rifle shot.

He had expected the German artillery, which he could now identify as 5.9 cm close support guns, to open fire at once. Instead, the three tanks came grinding forward slowly until they reached a dip in the ground, where they halted. Groups of infantry came on past them, advancing in short dashes along the fringe of the trees.

In the forward slit trenches, the British troops waited until the enemy had come within a hundred yards. Then, with devastating effect, they opened fire. The Germans quickly withdrew, leaving a number of dead behind them. Then the enemy artillery opened up with a sustained and accurate artillery barrage.

The next attack came from the high ground above the river, the Germans seeking to turn the flank of the defences. It was beaten off, but only at the cost of heavy casualties to the British.

Through his binoculars, Stavely saw more enemy troops emerging from the woods, and knew that the Germans were committing everything they had to an all-out assault on Kvam before it grew dark. There was little he could do but pray for a miracle.

It came in a thunder of engines, just as the enemy opened up with a renewed artillery barrage. Sweeping across the mountains, in two tight formations, came a dozen Skua dive-bombers. They seemed to know exactly where the enemy positions were. One by one, they peeled off and screamed down in their characteristic steep dive, each releasing a couple of 250 lb bombs before flattening out. Geysers of smoke, dirt, snow and fragments of trees erupted from the spot where the German guns were situated. Some of the aircraft dropped their bombs right on top of the enemy tanks, two of which were blown upside down. The third beat a hasty retreat, reversing into the shelter of the trees. Then, in turn, the Skuas dived down and strafed the enemy troops, driving them back along the river bank.

As they formed up and flew away towards the coast, the pilot of the leading aircraft glanced back at the columns of smoke their bombs had created and smiled to himself. There was no greater satisfaction, thought Dickie Baird, than that which comes from a good job well done.

The train made its way slowly through the wreckage of Aandalsnes, finally drawing to a halt in a railway siding close to the harbour. Armstrong and Kalinski climbed down and watched as Norwegian troops marched off with the sullen-faced German prisoners.

Captain Jensen also watched them go, his face split by a broad grin as he spotted a man approaching. The two shook hands warmly, and Armstrong noticed that the newcomer was a civilian. After exchanging some words with Jensen, he approached the two pilots and extended his hand to them, too.

"Gentlemen," he said in cultured English, "I should like to introduce myself to you. My name is Arne Oftedahl, of the Norwegian Foreign Office. You have risked your lives to assist us in our little subterfuge, and my country is grateful to you."

"Subterfuge?" Armstrong was as perplexed as his fellow pilot. "I'm afraid I don't understand."

"No," Oftedahl smiled, "I don't suppose you do. Come with me, please."

He led them to the train, and a Norwegian soldier,

obeying his command, slid open the door of one of the freight cars. They clambered inside, and stood looking at several wooden crates lying tightly up against one another. Oftedahl looked around, and his gaze fell on an axe fastened to a wall close to the door; Norwegian wood-burning trains were well-equipped with such implements.

He tore it from its clips and swung it hard, its sharp blade shattering the lid of one of the wooden boxes. Pulling aside the splintered wood, he straightened up and gestured to Armstrong and Kalinski.

"Go ahead," he invited smilingly. "Help yourselves to Norway's gold."

With some hesitation, Kalinski reached down and groped inside the remains of the crate. A moment later he turned to face Armstrong, an expression of utter bewilderment on his face as he hefted the bar that was in his hands.

"Lead," he murmured. "It's lead. Just what in the name of heaven is going on?"

"I shall explain," Oftedahl said. "We were betrayed, you see. The traitor Quisling and his friends informed the enemy that we planned to move the gold to England. We knew that the Germans would do their utmost to seize it, so we let it slip that we were going to ship it out via Aandalsnes. We hoped that we would draw considerable enemy forces into this area, temporarily diverting the enemy's attention from operations that were taking place elsewhere. I'm afraid that we had to mislead a number of people in the interests of security, including Colonel Gough, Captain Jensen

– and, of course, yourselves. I regret this very much, but it was necessary."

"I'll be damned," Armstrong said, with considerable feeling. So where *is* the gold?"

"The shipment was switched at Lillehammer," Oftedahl told him. "It was then transported to another small port north of Namsos, one so unimportant that the Germans wouldn't bother with it, and there it was transferred to a British cruiser. Only the highest-ranking Norwegian and British officials knew about the scheme. As an added bonus, the British Admiralty arranged for an aircraft-carrier to be standing by off Aandalsnes, with orders for its aircraft to attack the enemy forces which we knew would be searching for the train. I understand that they have already been in action, in support of British and Norwegian troops at Kvam."

Armstrong looked him in the eye. "I understand everything you've said. But tell me – it seems you've gone to an awful lot of trouble to safeguard the gold shipment. After all, it could have been taken off at Aandalsnes, couldn't it?"

Oftedahl shook his head. "The risk was considered too great. You see, when the gold left Lillehammer it had an important travelling companion. At this very moment, *en route* to safety in England with his family and the gold, is His Majesty King Haakon of Norway."